Through working in hairdressing for many years, Carole Lonsdale has listened to things clients have opened up to her about intimate experiences, heartbreak, and mental health problems, all of this has been stored inside her brain, and this is how this book has emerged.

I dedicate this to my family, encouraging me to put pen to paper and release all that has been stored inside my head.

Carole Lonsdale

THE BITCH IN DISGUISE

AUSTIN MACAULEY PUBLISHERS®

LONDON • CAMBRIDGE • NEW YORK • SHARJAH

A CIP catalogue record for this title is available from the British Library.

ISBN 9781035877362 (Paperback)
ISBN 9781035877379 (ePub e-book)

www.austinmacauley.com

First Published 2024
Austin Macauley Publishers Ltd®
1 Canada Square
Canary Wharf
London
E14 5AA

To my husband and family, for encouraging me to put pen to paper and release all the innermost thoughts stored inside my head.

Table of Contents

They call her the Bitch in Disguise
She gives a smile, looks them straight in the eyes
Two faces she knows how to portray
That innocent smile on her face will stay

She knows things are said behind her back
And will make you the Bitch if you attack
She thinks she will never be caught out
Be warned, lock up, your man when she is about.

She is everybody's friend, gives you all her attention till she digs and roots out as much information and everything about you, then when your usefulness is all used up your dumped on the scrap heap so she can move on to her next vulnerable unsuspecting victims.

Elisa is nothing spectacular, not the sort of person you would pass in the street and think, *Wow what a stunner, no but she does have the gift of the Gab and calls herself very flirty.*

When she enters your life, she is like a blood-sucking leech, she will text you and make continuous phone calls asking for your company, till she starts to get bored and feels the need to manipulate people of both sexes into her lair.

She is obsessed with sex and can't stop talking about all her sexual experiences and conquests from the age of seven years when she had her first fumble with her cousin which later resulted in regular sex.

She goes on to tell, about her lunchtime meetings behind the bike sheds at school and how on a school trip she purposely left her bag on the coach made an excuse to the teacher to go back for it and had sex on the back seat with the coach driver. This resulted in her being expelled from school.

Elisa was the youngest child from a family of six; she states her parents were quite strict with her, at the age of sixteen she met her first serious boyfriend he was nineteen and lived in a bedsit, she would make excuses to stay over with him by telling her parents she was staying with a girlfriend, but one evening, she was nearly caught out as her father went to the girl's house and found she was not there and had not even made arrangements to see the friend. Her father went round to her boyfriend's flat and was banging on the door; she saw it was her father and managed to get out of a window to hide, the boyfriend opened the door and assured him she was not there and he could see for himself.

She wanted to stay with her boyfriend as much as possible to satisfy her lust for sex; on approaching the age of eighteen they asked her parents if they could get married, so after a small register office wedding, they set up a home together and then a short while after, she found she was pregnant with her first child.

They could no longer stay at the bedsit and were lucky enough to be given a council house and at nineteen, she gave birth to a son.

Being a mum for the first time she had the opportunity to meet up with other mothers at the local clinic and baby clubs. She secured friendships with not only the mums but also the husbands and partners; they started to arrange parties and meetings at each other's homes.

Through all these social meetings, an affair was on the horizon, and it happened to be with her friend's husband who lived at the house that backed on to the bottom of their garden with easy access.

The man called Bob worked shifts as did his wife at different times which made it possible to meet after her husband left for work.

She was getting more and more frustrated with her own husband; she wanted the excitement of a new man in her life and a secret illicit affair.

They arranged they would meet in the garden shed, she arrived wearing skimpy shorts, no bra and a flimsy top.

As she walked inside, she took off her top; he was there waiting for her and his manhood was rapidly rising. She removed her shorts and fell to her knees and took his throbbing penis into her mouth; Bob was moaning with ecstasy; he then withdrew and threw her down on to the floor and started to massage and suck her breasts, bringing her groaning and pleading for him to enter her.

The affair went on for months, secret meetings when their partners were out of the way. One afternoon, Elisa's husband Jack unexpectedly came home from work to find she was not at home. He tried to contact her but there was no answer from her phone; he went to the neighbour's house but nobody answered the door; little did he know she was having sex in the garden shed with his friend.

He then thought she must be round at her parent's home so he decided to go and see if she was there. When he arrived, he heard the child in the garden and sure enough, the grandparents were playing with him but there was no sign of Elisa.

He asked where she was and they looked surprised and said they thought he knew she brought Tommy around to them for a few hours while she helped a friend with a disability. Jack looked surprised and said she had not mentioned it to him.

He then told them the reason he was sent home was because he had been made redundant. Things now were certainly going to be different till he could find another job.

A while later, Elisa arrived to collect Tommy and was shocked to see Jack sitting there. He started to explain what had happened, why he was home early and how worried he was about finding another job as it was not going to be easy.

He then asked about the friend she was helping the one with the disability; Elisa was trying to stay calm but started stuttering and stammering while trying to make her lies sound true and convincing.

She said he did not know the person; it was through a friend of a friend that she said she would help with some cleaning and shopping; she thought to herself, *Thank God, Jack believed me.*

Now she would not be able to see her lover as much as she would have liked and would just have to be content with her husband.

Months went by with no sign of work for Jack and very few secret meetings with her lover.

Frustrations and boredom were taking over her life; she wanted more excitement. When one morning she woke up feeling very sick, she thought that she had picked up a bug, days went by and feeling no better, she thought to do a pregnancy test and yes it came back positive.

This was not the news she wanted but told Jack and he was over the moon with the news, but she made him promise not to say anything not even to her parents as she said it was still early days. They realised their finances would be stretched even further with another mouth to feed and their son Tommy starting nursery.

Elisa was thinking of those few months of freedom when she had been able to meet up with her lover but with two children, it would not be so easy. She was not going to tell him about her pregnancy.

One morning, Jack had a phone call to ask if he was interested in a short contract, some work had come up but it would mean him being away from home for at least three months. He spoke to Elisa and decided because of the dire straight of their finance, he would accept the position.

That weekend, he packed his clothes and made his way to his new residence, both Elisa and Tommy were sad to see him go, but she also thought that she had freedom once again to see her lover.

After Jack had left, she had to think of a good excuse to get Bob to come over to her house. She phoned her friend giving a sob story that she felt something had gone wrong in the loft and would it be possible for Bob to come and have a look.

Her friend said that she would get Bob to come and see if he could sort it out for her; she was so trusting that she had no clue what was going on between them.

The little boy was tucked up in bed fast asleep when Bob knocked on the door, and she was ready and waiting in her sexy dressing gown and underneath her red camisole.

She came through with two glasses of wine at the ready, He shouted, "Hi, Elisa," then dropped his toolbox, and stood there looking at her as she let her dressing gown slip to the floor exposing her still slim body.

With his insatiable hunger and need for her, he lifted her on to the table and took her Elisa willingly surrendering her body to satisfy her own needs.

They were both in their own world when the phone started ringing; thinking it might be Jack, Elisa answered to find it was Cathy, Bob's wife wanting to know if Bob had found what the problem was and had he sorted it and when he was coming home.

The next day, Jack phoned to say he had been offered an extension to his contract, the money was too good to refuse and he would not be returning till her seventh month of pregnancy, and would not be able to get home for weekends. This of course gave her more freedom but she assured him she loved and missed him and would phone frequently.

Elisa in her head started to think about what her next move would be. Jack safely away meant she would be able to make more secret meetings with Bob. But she had to be careful as she did not want to create any suspicions towards Bob's wife, so she continued to be friendly and meet up with her and her other friends trying to keep things normal with their girlie chats. But once again, she was getting hungry for sex and excitement again with Bob.

She was now well into her fifth month of her pregnancy but still did not show and family and friends did not know she was pregnant.

Bob was controlled by his need for Elisa and would move mountains to be with her, when they met up, she told him she wanted more excitement no more quickies in the garden shed. She wanted to be wined and dined to stay over in a hotel, and not to be worried if Bob's wife was to come home early and catch them.

She said she would arrange with her parents to have the little boy for the weekend, she would tell them an old school friend had come over from Canada and had arranged a get-together with some other friends for them all to meet up. Her parents fell for it and told her to go and have a good time.

Bob also came up with a convincing story for his wife and told her he was going to a motorbike show; it was on for two days and he would have to stay over.

Elisa also phoned Jack and told him the same story and for him not to phone; she would contact him when she got back home and would tell him all about her weekend with her school friend, again she was so convincing that he believed her and because she was further into her pregnancy, he just said be careful and enjoy yourself.

With all the arrangements put in place, her son settled at grandparents, she started for the weekend, but all did not go to plan, on the journey down on the motorway, she was held up for three hours due to a crash. She decided to pull off at the next slip road and make her way through the country lanes that would take her in the direction of the secluded hotel they had booked.

Bob was at this stage starting to get concerned as he had not managed to get hold of Elisa on the phone; she was heading as she thought in the right direction down a narrow country lane; she had a puncture. With nobody in sight and her temper getting frayed, she got out of the car to try to phone for help but could not pick up a signal. Not knowing where she was and feeling very tired, she started to walk down the lane when she heard a noise coming towards her; it was a herd of cows and there was not much room for her to move out of the way. She then saw two men and started to scream at them, the one man sensing the danger managed to steer them in another direction across the road and into a field. Elisa had never been so terrified and relieved when they came up to ask if she was alright, seeing how distressed she was they suggested taking her to the farm house to calm her and give her a cup of tea. She was so grateful that she did not refuse and they also sorted out the tyre on her car so she could continue her journey.

She finally arrived at the hotel hours later and Bob was anxiously waiting for her, but what he saw, he realised how exhausted she was. There was not going to be any rapid lovemaking, instead, all she wanted was a long soak in the bath and a lie down where she fell asleep.

Later, she dressed and they went down together for the evening meal; she was sitting at the table waiting for Bob to return with drinks from the bar when she felt the presence of someone standing behind her.

The husky male voice said laughingly, "It's Elisa Ding Dong Bell, it is you." With a start, she turned to see a handsome guy standing behind her smiling.

She thought to herself *I don't know you.* Then he spoke and said remember middle school behind the bike sheds and was laughing.

A memory suddenly hit her and she blushed looking at him now and thinking about him then, he was a skinny spotty-faced kid who had been after her at school and she gave him a treat in the lunch hour in the long grass behind the bike shed.

But wow, just look at him now, she was thinking, he looked as if he did weight training and what a handsome guy.

Bob was on his way back from the bar with the drinks and she was thinking what do I say, but also thinking I would like to get to know you better and catch up on old times.

He said his name was Tony and that they would talk again before she left the hotel.

Then Bob started talking, but she felt it was going over her head, her heart was still racing from the meeting with Tony.

They had their meal and headed back to the room; Bob was full of expectations; he was feeling very arduous and wanted her to get undressed; he began roughly unzipping her dress, Elisa tried to play her part but her mind now was on Tony and thinking about those innocent days at school.

Bob could feel her reluctance and questioned what was wrong, she told him the weekend had not turned out as she thought it would and the disastrous start, and then she broke down something she did not often do, especially in front of Bob.

She then dropped the bombshell to him that she was pregnant, before she could sob any more, he took her in his arms and said he was happy, about the baby, and he would leave his wife and look after her the baby and her son.

Elisa found herself shouting, "No, Bob, no, it's not your baby; it is Jack's and he knew about it before he went away to work." Bob felt broken; he truly believed the baby to be his and he also wanted out of his marriage.

This news that Elisa wanted to stay with Jack was not what he was expecting; he had hoped the weekend together would make her feel she wanted to be with him. They lay on the bed and not touching each other.

The next day, they decided to leave early and make their way back to their homes; they said goodbye and went their separate ways.

But Elisa had one more thing she had to do before she left; she wrote a letter to Tony and asked at reception for it to be handed to him.

Returning Home

Bob needed to see Elisa as their parting had been severely strained; he could not text or phone in case his wife got hold of his phone. He wanted answers as to why she had not mentioned her pregnancy and had kept it secret; he still thought the baby could be his; it was a continuous nagging torment inside his head; he could not concentrate on his work and Cathy, his wife was starting to notice how unsettled he was, when she questioned him to see if he was alright, he told her it was the pressure of work, but in reality, he wanted to be with Elisa and was preparing to leave his wife and family.

Elisa was now into the seventh month of her pregnancy but outwardly still did not show, it would be only another few weeks till Jack returned home and was thinking about how things were going to change when he came back; she would no longer have her freedom that she had become accustomed to over the last few months.

The phone started ringing; thinking it was Jack, she ran to answer it but all she heard on the other end was sobbing and a voice saying, "Elisa, what am I going to do? Bob wants to leave me."

In shock, Elisa tried to pacify her friend and said, "Cathy, what are you talking about? Have you had another argument?" Cathy was near to hysteria saying Bob had told her that he had met another woman; he no longer loved her and wanted to move in with her. He would not tell her who she was. Elisa tried to comfort her and said that when she took her son to nursery, she would come over.

Panic set in; what was she going to say; she kept hoping Bob would be at work, yet she needed to see him to see he was not in a state and going to tell all about their affair.

That morning she arrived at Cathy's house to find her still uncontrollably crying and saying over and over again, "Why why?" She said like many of their friends, they had arguments usually over finances. But they got on well and things were good in bed, although she did think Bob had been a bit distant recently but had put it down to the pressure of his work.

Elisa just sat there listening and let her friend cry it out; she tried to encourage her saying maybe it was just a phase and Bob would come to his senses; she tried to sound convincing yet her own heart was racing ten to a dozen in sheer panic in case Bob came in and told all.

She looked at her watch and made the excuse that it was time to fetch her son from nursery.

As she was about to get into her car, Bob arrived in his van, he got out and came over saying, "I need to see you." She told him she had been with Cathy and she was broken-hearted. She pleaded with him not to tell off their affair and would arrange to meet him later so they could talk.

A few hours later, an anxious Elisa met up with Bob in a secluded lane. Bob had parked his van and came over to her, they talked for a while in her car; Bob was getting more and more distraught so she suggested they go for a walk.

He then turned and took her in his arms saying, "I can't go on without you and will leave Cathy." He kept insisting the baby was his and why would she not admit it. He said, "You know you get more excitement with me than you do with Jack and we must get away together."

Elisa was trying to keep control and kept insisting the baby was Jack's and after the birth, she said, to pacify Bob, maybe they could sort things and get away.

Bob turned to her with a savage look on his face; he grabbed her and threw her to the ground saying, "I need you now." His eyes looked strange; he was breathing heavily; he unzipped his trousers. Elisa feeling fearful now was pleading with him and feeling helpless to try to calm him. Bob took no notice; he pushed up her skirt, ripped off her panties and roughly took her, no tenderness this time; this was a different tormented Bob.

Elisa shocked at what had just happened put her clothes back on and made to move back to her car leaving Bob sitting there with his head in his hands.

Elisa was obviously distressed by what had just taken place and made her way to her parents to pick up her son and tried to act normal, but her mother sensed something was not right and asked what was the matter. Elisa tried to put on a front by saying she had a bad day consoling a friend who was going through a marriage breakdown and the strain had taken its toll on her. After a catchup with her parents, she and her son made their way back home. All she wanted to do now was settle Little Tommy, have a long soak in the bath and go to bed.

The phone was ringing; feeling uneasy about who it was and wondering if it was Bob, she hesitantly answered to an excited Jack, her husband, who could not wait to tell her the work he had been doing was now finished and at the end of the month, he would be back home.

Suddenly Elisa started to cry. She said through her sobs that she had been through a stressful day; she explained she had been comforting a friend without going into too much detail, and said she would be glad when he came back home. She was also thinking that they could not stay in this house; she must try and put pressure on Jack for them to look for another home. She went off to bed feeling some relief that her husband would soon be back home but thoughts were swirling around inside her head.

In the early hours, she woke up in pain and felt the bed wet; she panicked she was in labour and it was too early; she frantically phoned her parents who came to collect Tommy and to wait till the ambulance arrived. She was so worried as she was only seven months into her pregnancy and was wondering if was it the way Bob had viciously used her that started it off; the labour was long and painful but she eventually gave birth to another son. The baby was tiny and had difficulty breathing and was taken to a special baby unit as he was only 4lb in weight.

She was so exhausted and after managing a few hours of sleep, she woke to find Jack at her side smiling but with a worried look.

He told her the baby was in intensive care because he was so tiny and because of his breathing. Jack was allowed to take Elisa in a wheelchair so that she could see the baby through a window; he looked so tiny lying there and was attached to tubes which sent fear racing through her. Because the birth had been so traumatic, she also had to stay longer in the

24

hospital and the baby who they named Jimmy after Jack's dad was also kept in the hospital for a couple of months.

This gave Elisa extra time away from Bob and for her to put pressure on Jack to move to another home.

She was lucky she had not bumped into Cathy or Bob; excuses were made by Jack that she was told she had to rest up and because she was visiting the hospital daily to express milk for the baby.

She was getting used to having Jack back at home all the time; there was no sign of work, and with two children, money matters were going to be difficult, they would even have to cut back on Little Tommy's nursery. This is why she was hoping they could move nearer to her parents hoping they could help to look after the children and she was pleasantly surprised when Jack agreed that it would be a good idea.

Home from Hospital

Finally, Elisa and Jack were told the baby was responding well and putting on weight and they would be able to take him home. Jack came to the hospital to pick them both up and took them to Elisa's parents so they could meet their new grandson, both they and Little Tommy were so excited to see the new addition to the family; lots of fuss was made of mother and baby when suddenly Elisa's father said, "Can't see who this little fellow looks like, maybe someone down the family line." With that, Elisa started coughing and choking and her mum ran to fetch her a glass of water; with that she regained control; she timidly laughed and said maybe he resembled their family who went to Australia and they had not heard from them for years. With that, her dad said, "Yes, you could be right."

Jack did not say anything and just joined in laughing, but Elisa was thinking *Oh my God is this Bob's son*? She knew then she would have to put an end to the affair, and work on Jack more to move to a new home.

When they arrived back home, the phone was ringing and it was Cathy asking if she could pop around to see the baby. She in the beginning kept making excuses that she was not well or that something was wrong with the baby, anything she could think of to put her friend off seeing the child.

She was so grateful that Bob had not tried to contact her since that night when she went into labour. Jack had spoken to Bob in the garden and explained how difficult things were for Elisa, but did not mention they were hoping to move.

Bob was getting frustrated as it was now over two months since he last saw Elisa; he wanted to tell her how sorry he was for what had taken place that last night they met. He was still very unhappy with his marriage and still wanted out but knew he could not just walk away as he had nowhere to go.

In his head, he was still living in the dream that Elisa wanted to make plans for their future together.

Little Jimmy was nearly three months old when Elisa went into the nursery to check on him and found him struggling to breathe; she screamed and Jack came running in took hold of the baby told her to call for an ambulance. The little fellow was rushed to hospital where they found he had a severe chest infection and again had to stay in hospital.

Elisa went in daily as she was still breastfeeding and had to express her milk; it was over three weeks that he was kept in the hospital till they felt he was well enough to return home.

During that time, Elisa was putting more pressure on Jack to look for another home, when one morning her mother phoned to say she had been talking to a neighbour about them wanting to move and she knew of a friend who also wanted to move to the area where Elisa lived.

They arranged to meet up and view the homes and both decided they would like to swap, so arrangements were made through the council and Elisa and Jack finally moved to their new home.

Elisa had still not seen Bob but had spoken to Cathy on the phone, and explained about how ill the baby had been; sorry they could not catch up as they were busy getting settled with the move taking place so quickly and that it was going to be closer to her parents and that they would be able to help to look after the children as she was hoping to go back to work as Jack had still been unable to find anything since his contract had finished. She was hoping between nursery and her parents, she could go back to her line of work as a mobile beautician. In her mind, that would give her the chance to meet the Ding Dong man Tony whom she had left a note at the hotel and he had recently contacted her. Cathy said she understood and was sorry that they were leaving and could meet up for a coffee and chat when they had settled.

The Mobile Business

After the move to their new home, Jack and Elisa settled into the new routine quickly, and as Jack was a very good handyman who set out to modernise the home, fitting a kitchen and bathroom and extensively decorating throughout the home kept him very busy.

Elisa had arranged with the grandparents for them to help with childcare as she had also decided to try to work for herself as a mobile beautician and was fortunate that through friends and previous clients was able to build up a good circle of clients and appointments were well underway which left little time to think of anything else.

Jack was happy and when friends saw what he had achieved at the house, they asked him why didn't he work for himself; so after some discussion, he also set about to prepare to start his own business.

Both were kept very busy which meant they did not see a lot of each other, only certain evenings at home as Elisa went out to party make-up evenings bringing in extra income.

Elisa's body after the birth and all the work she had been doing was now getting back to normal again and she was starting to get sexually frustrated. She decided she would arrange a meeting with Tony but away from the hotel.

She and Tony met up at a little country pub where no one knew her; they chatted over the old days at school and how life had treated them; she found out Tony had been married but his wife had run off with another woman, and now he found it hard to trust anyone. He was so sincere and she felt an attraction towards him. The time had flown by while they were chatting and she said to Tony that they must meet up again and in the near future, no mention was made of Bob or the weekend at the hotel which left her feeling relieved.

That first meeting made her feel so sexually attracted to Tony that when they said their goodbyes, he gave her a long lingering kiss; she was thinking, please another meeting soon.

When she arrived back home, good reliable Jack had given the children their tea and settled them in bed and was now dozing on the settee in front of the T.V. She gently woke him up, saying "I am back and it's time for bed."

Both businesses were thriving and things looking up. Jimmy was getting stronger but still did not look like any member of the family. Jack was oblivious to that; just happy that his son was getting on and doing the normal things that babies did. Thankfully, she was so busy with work that she did not have time to go to the mother and baby groups or meet up with old friends and neighbours so no one had met little Jimmy.

She did have a meeting with her friend Cathy for coffee when out shopping and asked how everyone was doing and casually asked how was Bob, to which she replied she was still fighting to save her marriage but Bob always seemed distracted. Consoling her friend and then changing the subject saying they would all have to try to get together and have a girlie night out; they then said their goodbyes and went their separate ways.

Elisa was inwardly congratulating herself on how she had handled the situation with Cathy and was thankful Bob had not tried to contact her. She was hoping that just maybe his feelings towards her were starting to fade and cool off.

She then went to her parents to collect the children but before going home, she would give them a treat and go to the park where they could play for a while.

She was sitting watching the children when she heard a voice shout, "Hi. Elisa, are you OK?" She turned and saw Bob going slowly past in his van and he shouted, "Can't stop." She smiled and waved but was visibly shaken; she did not think he would still have that effect on her, and with that, she got the children back into the car and went home.

Jack arrived a few minutes later and was excited and said, "I have got some good news." A friend passed on the word about Jack's work and an associate in London wanted to know if he would be interested in renovating a flat for him; it was too good to turn down but meant being away from home for a while and estimated about a month. Elisa had been used to Jack working away and said it would be alright, she had her work and the children to see too.

Later that week, Elisa had a call to go to do a treatment and was told the person had a disability and would that be alright. She had not been to this flat before and when she arrived, the door was opened by a young boy who looked about 15 years old; he said, "Come in and set your things up." Then he went to another room and she heard him say, "The lady is here. I am off now."

Elisa was preparing her table and equipment when she heard a voice say, "Hi, Elisa, long time, no see." She turned to see Bob standing in the doorway; she found herself feeling very flustered and her heart was racing and wondering what was going to happen next. She was not prepared for this Bob smiled and said, "I am so sorry, so very sorry for what happened the last time we met and this was the only way could think of to meet you again."

Elisa thought how tired and dejected Bob looked and her heart started to melt at the sight of him, she then looked at him and said, "I don't expect you will be wanting this treatment after all." With that, she went over to him and he took her in his arms her perfume and the feel of her were intoxicating and sent uncontrollable feelings through his body. Elisa did not say anything, just followed Bob's lead into the bedroom where he gently lifted her onto the bed. She did not resist as he removed her clothes, took her gently at first and then gave her what she really wanted. When they had finished their lovemaking, he turned and said to her, "Are we still on?"

Elisa knew Bob was good and gave her what she wanted to satisfy her needs, but what was she doing Bob was a ticking time bomb and could blow open everything about their affair. She knew she would have to tread carefully and keep him happy for the time being.

Bob arrived home to find Cathy talking to her friend and overheard her say, "The baby does not look like either Jack or Elisa." Bob then questioned Cathy about what she was talking about with her friend and she said the friend had met Elisa's mum walking with the baby; they got chatting and she said she could see no resemblance to either of them. This made

Bob think again *was the child his, but how was he going to get the proof he needed*?

An opportunity arose for Bob; the company he worked for as a plumber called him in to go and do a service on a boiler and heating system; he did not realise it was Elisa's parent's home till he arrived there as he had only seen them once when they came to visit at the old house.

He casually said to her mother when asked if he would like a drink, he said, "I recognise you. Are you my old neighbour's parents?"

The mum answered saying, "What a coincidence and yes that's right." Bob then asked how they both were in their new home; she replied saying they were fine and Elisa had another son and they looked after him a few days a week so she could go out to work; he was with them now, and with that, the door opened and her husband was standing with the baby in his arms.

Bob stopped work to have a cup of tea and it gave him a chance to look at the child; he saw no resemblance to Jack or Elisa but when the baby chuckled and smiled, he could see a resemblance to his own brother. He now had to manage to get a DNA test; the problem was going to be how and when.

Bob got a test kit and kept it with him so that Cathy would not get suspicious. Weeks went by; he had not even seen Elisa since the meeting at the flat. It was just work and more and more frustration because he could not get the information on the baby, he was now calling his son.

Then a stroke of luck; when he went to work, he was given the address of Elisa's parents, again to go to repair a leak. He had the kit ready in case there was an opportunity to take a sample.

The leak was not a straightforward job and would take some time to repair. He went into the kitchen and the little fellow was sitting in his high chair and not very happy whimpering and dribbling; his grandmother said he was teething.

Next thing, the doorbell was ringing and she went to answer it, as quickly as he could, Bob sped into action, got the kit out went over to the little boy and managed to get a sample of saliva, put it back into the tube and in his pocket as the grandmother came back through the door to find Bob standing next to the high chair talking to the little fellow, she smiled and said, "He seems to like you."

Bob then turned to repair the pipe; he was feeling quite excited that he had managed to get the test and would get it away as soon as possible and await the result.

A week later, the result arrived; with trembling fingers, he opened the envelope and it read there was a high per cent positive that he was the father. So now he would have to meet up with Elisa.

Bob was elated over the result of the test that he now had a son and with Elisa; now she would leave Jack and would want to be with him and realise they were meant to be together.

After a difficult week trying to contact Elisa, he was finally able to arrange a meeting but did not tell her about the test as he wanted to see her reaction as he showed her the result.

That evening, Elisa was preparing herself to meet Bob oblivious to what was to come; she was thinking it was a couple of months since they had last met and she had also not seen Cathy to catch up on how the situation was at home. She was quite excited about having a few hours with Bob as they still had that spark for each other and there had been no harassment about the child.

She told Jack she would be late home as she was doing a beauty evening for a hen party.

She then set off to meet Bob at his friend's flat; he told her he was out of the country for a few weeks and had been asked to do some work on the flat for him, hence that was how they could meet up there without anyone seeing them. As she entered the flat, she noticed how sexy Bob was looking; she could smell his familiar aftershave; he had drinks waiting for her and the lighting was dimmed. She could feel herself getting sexually excited just by his presence and she made her way over to him, the old feelings were still there and it was good.

He was not going to rush things and would not spoil the moment by mentioning the test. He handed her a glass of champagne and steered her over to the sofa.

She then commented, "Wow, Bob, splashing out on champers, what is the celebration!"

With a husky voice and full of emotion, he said, "You, my darling, it's so good to see you." With that, he took her in his arms and gently found her lips pushed open her mouth with his tongue he started to explore. He then unzipped her dress and started caressing and licking her breasts bringing on an ecstasy she fondly remembered, he then pulled her up letting her dress fall to the floor leaving her naked, throbbing with excitement and wanting more she helped to remove Bob's clothes, his head was thrown back moaning with sheer pleasure as she took his throbbing penis her mouth then down over her breasts and her belly and to her vagina frantically opening her legs for him to enter her and take her out of this world.

Later, they had a bath together and were thinking, *what a perfect few hours*. Elisa was putting on her clothes and ready to go home when Bob came up to her and said smiling, "I have something to show you."

She answered thinking he wanted more from her, "Don't you think you have had enough," and was laughing.

Bob's face was now serious and said, "When are you going to leave Jack and come and live with me?"

She looked at him and replied "You know I can't because of the baby," thinking that would pacify him.

Bob's tone changed and said, "There is no reason for you to stay with Jack; the baby is mine and here is the proof," as he showed her the paperwork.

Elisa was suddenly numb with shock could not find her voice and was thinking this couldn't be happening, all sorts were going through her mind, and how did he get the samples to do the test? She was holding the paperwork staring at where it said positive and thinking this could not be happening.

What will Bob do now? Will he tell everyone about the affair and blow it all into the open? She tried to be calm and spoke saying, "This is a shock, I can't take it all in; you must give me a few days to work things out." Hoping that would calm him and give her time, she agreed they would meet again at the flat to put things into action. Bob agreed to give her time and said he would not tell Cathy or anyone else till they could find somewhere for them to be together.

They then went their separate ways; Bob full of optimism, Elisa full of terror.

After a restless night wondering what next was about to happen, she heard through her brain fog Jack asking if she was alright and saying, "It must have been some hen party as you were shouting in your sleep but could not make out what you were saying." *Oh God*, she thought, *good job he could not understand what I was mumbling.* She told him it had been a late finish and she was feeling rather tired. She then got the children ready and took them off to school and nursery and said to Jack she would see him later and do a special meal as they had the evening together.

She could not tell Jack what was happening; it would break his heart as he thought the world of his children; he always had been a good husband to her and had always done his best to provide for the family.

She was racking her brains as to how she was going to deal with the situation with Bob as now he knew the child was his; it was now beyond reasoning with him, and what would she tell her parents; she could not confide in her friends who were also friends of Cathy and knew Bob was having an affair.

They all knew Elisa was a flirt but did not point the finger her way. Bob had not confided in any of his male friends with whom he was having the affair and thought things with him and Cathy were slowly getting back on an even keel.

Elisa tried to take her mind off things by throwing herself into work and went off to an appointment with a new client, she was in the middle of a massage when the client's phone started ringing, she passed the phone to her and heard the lady say, "Oh no, that is awful. When did it happen and is his wife alright? I will call and see Cathy later."

Elisa froze hearing the name Cathy and thinking it couldn't be the Cathy she knew and did not think this lady would know her. She came back to reality when she heard the lady say, "Is that it? Is my massage finished? I will have to get ready to go and see my friend as I have just heard the terrible news that her husband has been in a bad accident and is in hospital on life support."

Elisa felt her heart pounding; could this be Bob, she felt she could not question the lady so cleared away her equipment and when leaving said, "I hope your friend is alright."

She made her way home and did not hear anything from any of her other friends, did not tell Jack when he arrived home and he had not heard anything as he would have said. she thought it must be someone else with the name Cathy.

The next morning the phone rang and it was her mother saying, "You know the man that sorted out our plumbing, the one that said he knew you and Jack from your old home, well I have just heard he is critically ill in hospital after a horrendous accident."

Elisa dropped the phone and was shaking, she could hear her mother shouting, "Elisa, are you ok?"

She picked up the phone and said, "Yes, I dropped the phone and what a shock; they were good neighbours at the bottom of the garden but had not seen much of them since we moved, but I will try to contact Cathy, his wife."

Later when she felt more composed, she tried to ring Cathy but got no answer so assumed she would be at the hospital with Bob.

She suddenly felt the need to go to the hospital to see Bob for herself, but would they let her in, would Cathy be grateful for some company? But not having seen her friend for a while and not knowing if Bob had been conscious and had said anything or mentioned her name, she battled with herself not knowing what to do, also in her mind was what had Bob done with the DNA paperwork.

She started to hear from various people that Bob had sustained life-changing injuries and was in and out of consciousness.

Three weeks later, Cathy was on the phone crying and saying Bob had passed away but was also whispering their names Jack and Elisa before he died.

Elisa had to think quickly and said, "Oh, I expect it was when Bob was doing work for my parents and they were chatting about us being old neighbours and that could have been on his mind," thinking she had managed to get around that and she was also trying to console Cathy by saying if she needed help with arranging the funeral, she would be there for her.

After putting down the phone, she broke down letting the tears fall feeling sad for the loss of Bob and thinking of the times they had shared, and now had accepted that he was the father of her son; she also felt a sense of relief that now it would not come out into the open. But she still had to put on her other face to get through the funeral.

Later when Jack arrived home, he noticed, she had been crying, and asked why, she covered herself by saying she had been consoling Cathy, and it had hit her what would she do if she lost Jack. He then came over took her in his arms and said, "Don't worry, you know me, I am made of tough stuff." She thought then yes, good reliable Jack.

Four weeks later, it was the day of the funeral; they both attended, the service was a tribute to Bob saying he was a loving husband and family man. Elisa was inwardly cringing and was thinking of all the times they had spent together; she felt all eyes were on her, yet no one in their close circle of friends had any idea what had been going on with their affair they had covered their tracks well.

They both went back to the wake and knew she had to keep things normal; she went and hugged Cathy and then chatted to the others saying both she and Jack missed the company and the meetings they used to have, but with both their business, they found it hard to find time to socialise. She was so convincing her friends just said they must make time to get together and catch up.

So life went back to normal; she had her work and Jack was getting more and more well-known, but it did mean a lot of time, he could be away from home for weeks at a time. This was when Elisa's frustrations started to creep back in; she lacked the excitement in her life.

The children were getting older; they spent a lot of time with their grandparents or friends from school so she felt she was not needed as much. She tried to re-kindle some old friends and was still her old flirty self but now lacked her old pulling power; she felt she needed new pastures.

Although her work took her to meet people, men and women, there was no spark there with any of her clients; she was losing her touch. The only thing she could be thankful for was both businesses were doing well, which brought in a reasonable income to enhance their home and their way of living.

The Knock on the Door

The years flew by; Elisa kept busy with work and took her children to football clubs, and many other things they had joined, and this also gave her the chance to meet up with other families.

One morning after seeing the boys off to school, she settled down to have a coffee and was browsing her diaries and it suddenly hit her that it was four years since Bob died, she smiled thinking of the fond memories of the moments they had secretly snatched to be together and then she thought of her younger son, Bob's son, about his start in life and how he was growing into a lovely little boy and thank goodness he showed no resemblance to Bob.

She was in a dream mulling over these things when she heard a knock on the door. She was not expecting anyone and it was a cold wet day out there.

When she opened the door, she nearly fainted and had to hold on to the door frame for support, she was at a loss for words and just kept staring at the man in front of her.

The man said, "Hi, are you Elisa?" With that, she found her voice and answered shakily, "Yes." The man standing in front of her was the double of Bob, he then spoke saying, "I am sorry if I shocked you and caused you distress but I am

Bob's twin brother." With that, she said, "You had better come inside."

She noticed he was carrying a briefcase, she offered him a coffee so they could sit down and chat.

He introduced himself as Tony, Bob's twin and had been travelling with his work to different countries over the last ten years and had not been in touch with his brother. Mail had finally caught up with him and that was how he got to know about his brother's death, and had got a son.

Fear and anxiety shot through Elisa; how much had Bob told him about their affair? Tony seeing the look on her face said, "I know this must be a shock to you, me turning up like this." He said he had been to see Cathy but had not said anything to her about the information he held inside his briefcase; he said he just let Cathy talk about the affair Bob had been involved in but did not know who the person was; she told him he was about to leave her. Elisa let out a sob and was shaking, that was when Tony went over to her sat next to her, took her hand and said, "Don't worry, Bob said you made him very happy and he was proud when he knew he had a son." He then put his arms around her pulled her into an embrace and before long, they were kissing. Elisa suddenly felt safe as though she was in Bos's arms once again.

But little did she know what was in store. Tony released her and started to apologise, but said he would like to meet up with her again before he left the country and to discuss things about his brother.

Elisa said excitedly, "Yes, of course, we can." She also wanted to know how much he knew about the affair.

A week went by, she had no news from Tony, then into the second week, she arrived home to find a note pushed through her door asking her to meet him at the same address where she had met Bob.

Jack was away working; she arranged for the children to sleep over at the grandparents on the pretext of a girl's night away.

Full of excitement and anticipation, she got herself ready wearing the dress Bob had always liked; she felt good and looked good, it had been a long time since she had got ready for a date.

She decided she would take a taxi instead of her car as she did not want to be seen near the flat.

She arrived, rang the doorbell and waited; no one answered; she rang again thinking had she got the right day when suddenly the door opened but it was not Tony that stood there; again she thought *have I got the right flat?* Then the man said, "Elisa, come inside."

She suddenly felt fear and panic and managed to say, "Who are you? I arranged to meet Tony."

Then the man introduced himself and said, "I am Dan, a friend of Tony's," and said, "Come inside" and assured her Tony was there. He guided her through to the lounge and offered her a glass of champagne; Elisa sipped her drink and started to relax as Dan seemed friendly and had a wicked sense of humour and made her laugh; he offered her another glass and said Bob was on the phone and would be with her shortly.

She was now feeling slightly light-headed and thinking a glass of wine usually did not react to her this quickly.

Dan suddenly said to her, "I think it's time you come with me, Tony should be ready now." He took her through and opened the door to the bedroom where she saw Tony on the bed naked.

He then said, "Hi, Elisa." She could feel herself getting excited seeing him lying there holding his penis and said, "Come on, girl, you know you want this." In her head, she could see Bob lying there calling her over and telling her to take off her dress, she unzipped the dress, let it fall to the floor exposing her naked body. She made her way over to the bed and went astride Tony licking his body slowly till she reached his penis and took it into her mouth sucking and feeling the ecstasy rise in her body, she then sat astride Tony letting him lick and fondle her vagina, she was getting near her peak and had to have him inside her and was thrusting herself on him till Tony cried out and they both reached the peak together.

The next thing she felt was hands on her shoulders and it was not Tony; it was Dan saying, "It's my turn now." He turned her over and pushed his penis into her mouth and said, "Come on, suck, suck make it good."

She then felt Tony pull her back onto him, while Dan spread her legs and was sucking her vagina. Tony was massaging her breasts; she had never experienced anything like this before; two of them, it was mind-blowing. Dan then came to her and penetrated her thrusting slowly at first and then went wild; she felt herself shouting, "Bob, don't stop." She felt so exhilarated. Tony beneath her, Dan on top who had just reached his height; he withdrew and flopped to the side of the bed. She found herself in the middle of the two of them, still light-headed from the wine she fell asleep.

When she woke, the light was coming through the window, her head felt like lead, she thought she was back home, then looked around the room and it started to come back to her what had happened and it was not a dream, she realised she was naked and had arranged to meet Tony. She started to get up and her head was spinning and her body felt battered. She could hear no noise or movement from the other room; she picked up her dress, put it on and went to look for Tony as she went through the door, she thought, yes. there was another man.

Things started to come back to her, she thought about the drink; it must have been spiked. She looked in the bathroom, the lounge and the kitchen no sign of anyone, she found her coat and her shoes and made her way to the door where on the table lay a package with her name on it and a message that said, "This is for Bob's son and we will see you again."

She took hold of the package and made her way out of the flat; now she had to take a taxi back, she kept having flashbacks of what had happened in that bedroom, and thankfully, Jack would not be home for a few days.

The next day, her head became clearer and she started to realise just what had happened to her, and how she had been set up and used, but she could not tell anyone as she had no proof and had lied to her family about where she was supposed to be. The only thing she had was the wad of money the package that contained £2000, she could not prove there were two men that she had met Tony and Dan she was told, there was no trace of them even being at the flat.

She had a thought come to her as she had not seen Cathy for a while, she would call on the pretext of saying she was passing and thought she would call to see how she was coping since losing Bob.

She and Cathy were reminiscing over old times and the fun they all used to have with the get-togethers when Cathy said, "Oh, by the way, I had an unexpected visitor the other day, I was gobsmacked when I opened the door and it was Bob's twin brother, as we had not seen him for years, he and Bob had a falling out and lost touch with each other." She then said Steve had only just heard the news that had caught up with him about Bob's death.

Elisa drew in her breath and said, "What did you say his name was?" And once again she said, Steve. She then asked how long did he stay with you, to which Cathy replied and answered, "No, he said he was leaving the country the next day."

Elisa felt at a loss for words, did not know what to say in case she slipped up, but said, "What, after all, those years, he could only spend a few hours with you?"

"Yes," said Cathy, "but that was enough time spent with him as he is not a very pleasant man, so very different from my Bob."

Elisa made her excuses to leave and said, "We must catch up again and not leave it so long." She went on her way with more worries going around inside her head about what she had encountered with Tony and Dan, why the different names and what was he up to telling Cathy he was leaving the next day and yet it was a week later he had contacted her to make arrangements to meet at the flat, and said he would contact her again.

Another Shock

Elisa was walking through the door when she heard the phone ringing, thinking it was Jack, she ran to answer only to hear Cathy's voice asking if she was alright, what was she doing and how nice it would be to catch up, she said she now had another man come into her life and would like to introduce him to her friends, she was about to say goodbye when she suddenly said, "Oh, by the way, do you remember I told you Bob's twin brother arrived a few months ago, well, I have received a letter from a friend to say Steve had died in a road accident, and as he did not know who else to contact, he remembered he had been to see me and would forward on his will and other paperwork."

Elisa felt herself go into sheer panic about what would now come to light, she tried to keep her voice calm and said, "We will all have to get together when Jack comes back home."

Weeks went by; she felt herself getting bored with no excitement in her life, now the children were older, she saw less of the friends she used to have as they also were doing different things in their lives. And some had moved out of the area.

One day, when she was out shopping at her local supermarket, her mind on other things suddenly there was an almighty crash her trolley had caught an arrangement in the middle aisle and brought down a barricade of cans scattering them all over the floor; she heard a lady cursing on the other side and shouting can't you look where you are going.

When she looked, she recognised the woman as an old school friend; at first, they just looked at each other then started laughing and the woman called Jane said, "Elisa, you are still as clumsy as you used to be."

They had not seen each other since school days so they decided to have a coffee on and catch up on what each other had done in their lives since they left school. The conversation came around to Cathy and the loss of Bob, but Jane said, "It is good she has now met a new man and they were getting engaged."

"Yes," said Elisa, "we were chatting a few weeks ago but I did not know then she was getting engaged."

They looked at the time and said they had to get on their way but swapped phone numbers and said they would keep in touch.

Elisa arrived home to find Jack's van on the drive; she was surprised as she was not expecting him back home. When she entered, she saw him sitting in the chair looking tired and dejected. He told her he had called it a day on the work front as the customers had said they could not pay him as their business was in the hands of the receivers and there was no money to pay him. This was not the only company that he could not get payment for his work and he also had people demanding payments for the materials he had bought from them, but could not pay them, and did not know a way out of the situation.

Elisa only had little work not enough to pay the mortgage and other outgoings, things generally in the country were going into a recession and now the fear was are they going to lose their home, after a discussion they decided to put their house on the market and look for a smaller property.

Weeks turned into months with no sign of work and still no sale. Jack had to resort to signing on for benefits while looking for work; he walked around knocking on doors, but no hope was in sight.

Then one day out walking the dog, he met a friend he had not seen for years, told him what had happened and he was being pestered for money and was on the verge of going bankrupt; his friend said the place he worked at was looking for a labourer, would he be interested, why didn't he apply once he got his foot in the door, there may be other jobs come up.

The work was mainly sweeping up and various other jobs in the factory but he got it and it was work and he was again bringing in a wage; again he was able to pay the mortgage and the bills.

Elisa felt strange having Jack back at home and in bed every night; she still felt something may come to light about the affair with Bob and the other two men.

The months were flying by and it must have been about six months since she last saw Cathy and was wondering if she was still with the same man.

She heard the letterbox flap and thought it must be the post and went to collect a handful of letters which she dreaded as most were demanding money from them, she spotted a coloured envelope and thought what can this be. When she opened it was an invitation to Cathy's wedding in three weeks so she was still with this man. At least it was something to look forward to.

The day of the wedding finally arrived, Elisa was quite excited as it had been a while since she and Jack had been to an occasion together, Jack had told her to go and buy a new dress for the wedding even though the money had been quite an issue with them.

They decided to set off quite early as the little church was out in the country and had been difficult to find leading them to be late and arriving just a little ahead of the bride.

The church was full of a lot of their old friends, and people Elisa had not seen before; they managed to find seats at the back of the church and were able to see Cathy walking down looking radiant.

When the service was over and the couple were walking up the aisle, Elisa was distracted as she had dropped her purse and was kneeling to pick up her belongings and they were the last to leave the church.

When they got outside, there was no sign of the bride and groom as the photographer had whisked them away to the other side to take more pictures.

Elisa turned to Jack and said, "It could take hours and we will just be standing around so why don't we go back to the hotel where the reception is going to be held and wait for them there?" Jack not being overly keen on weddings agreed that would be a good idea. They found seats at the hotel, had a couple of glasses of wine and started to relax and enjoy each other's company just like old times.

A few hours later, Jack looked out of the window and saw the wedding party arrive and said to Elisa, "Let a few of them line up to meet the bride and groom and we can join the line later to introduce ourselves."

Elisa excused herself saying to Jack she was going to the ladies' room and would meet him by the door when the queue had reduced. They joined other friends and were chatting generally, as they came up to the couple and were about to shake hands when Elisa felt a cold shock go through her body and felt her legs go unstable and had to hold on to Jack. He said, "Are you alright?"

But she could not find the words, only to mumble, "I suddenly feel faint."

She heard Jack say, "Let's find a seat; it is most probably because you have not eaten and we had those drinks."

But Elisa's shock was she had come face to face with the other man she knew called Dan who drugged her and used her that night at the flat, and this was Cathy's new husband. She knew she would have to face him and see what his reaction would be towards her.

After a short while, she told Jack she was feeling better and should go into the reception. As they walked through, Cathy, the bride looked concerned and asked her friend if she was alright and then said, "Let me introduce you to my new husband."

Elisa looked straight at him but he showed no sign of recognising her at all, and just said he was pleased to meet them both and thanked them for coming to the wedding and then moved on to the next couple to greet them.

Elisa did not know how to react; she could not let Jack see that she was distressed so they made their way to the table amongst the other old friends and made the best of the situation, but inwardly she was thinking *what was this man who Cathy had just married up to and would he be in the future getting in touch with her?*

The bridal couple left the reception early as they had a plane to catch and off to their honeymoon, but as soon as they left, Elisa started to relax and enjoy the rest of the evening.

When they returned home, Elisa's mind started to work overtime, *what was going on what was this man Cathy's husband up to*? He held all the cards and all she could do now was wait for him to make his next move, but in the meantime, she could not let Jack know what was worrying her.

It had now been 18 months since Cathy's wedding and not many of their friends or ourselves had heard anything from her, till one evening the phone rang and it was Cathy sounding very happy and excited to tell us that she was pregnant and was expecting a son.

She said she had not been able to be in touch as they had been travelling the world with her husband's work, but were back home and expecting to stay till the baby was born, and how good it would be to have a catch up with the old crowd her women friends.

Arrangements were made to have a gathering at her house a week later as her husband Ian had to go to India for three months to do his work.

All the ladies arrived with gifts for the baby and wanted to get all the news on her husband and their travels. The afternoon went well and Cathy informed them she would be selling the house as they were planning to buy a house in America and needed the money to finance it.

Elisa suddenly felt warning bells ringing, knowing what she did to this man who now called himself Ian, she also thought listening to Cathy's tone that she did not feel a hundred per cent that she was doing the right thing about leaving her friends and family.

The more Elisa met up with Cathy over the next couple of weeks, she felt something was not quite right.

Cathy's house sold quickly and she was getting pressure to send the money over to secure the house or they would lose it, she had to take a rented flat and Ian assured her he would send for her as soon as it was settled.

She was coming into her sixth month of the pregnancy and had been having a bit of a rough time, the calls from her husband were getting fewer and she was starting to worry about what was going on, when he did speak to her, he said things were going through and everything going to plan.

But she had a shock coming; everything was going to plan for him; he had taken her money and there was no house. He had moved from the address he had given her and had changed the phone number. She had lost her home and with a baby on the way, did not know what to do, she informed the police, but there seemed little they could do.

A few weeks later before the baby was born, she received a letter from a lady in India who claimed to be Ian's wife and had three children with him, and that he had disappeared, she had found a letter with Cathy's address on it.

Not only was she heartbroken, she had lost her home and he had taken her money, but now to find out she was not legally married to that man.

Elisa felt so bad for her friend, because of what was happening and also because she had an affair with her husband.

But she was also thinking and breathing a sigh of relief, *surely this man Ian would not show his face again, and she could rest with the thought he would not try to contact her again.* And just maybe he had not got a copy of the DNA report on her son.

The Years Were Flying By

The years were flying by; the children were growing up and doing their own thing.

Elisa had been in and out of different jobs over the years due to a recession and had been cutting back on beauty treatments, and now she had not got an excuse to go out in the evenings telling Jack she was doing make-up parties as most of her friends and clients had moved on to other areas.

She had lost touch with Cathy after the baby was born as she could not manage after the break-up of her marriage that had not been legal and it resulted in her having a breakdown. Her parents came and took the family back to Ireland to live with them.

Elisa found part-time work in a local supermarket to help supplement their income, but one day at work while sitting at the till, she turned and felt something go in her back, resulting in time off and eventually having to go on disability benefits. By now, she was so bored with her own company and had a lot of problems with her own marriage to Jack.

She was out one day doing her daily walk with her dog when she heard her name being called, she turned to see an old school friend who she had not seen since school days, and they got chatting; she was being told by this friend that she and her husband had just moved back to the area and it would be lovely to catch up.

She arranged for her and her husband to come for a meal and to meet Jack.

She went home full of excitement and when Jack came home, she told him about the meeting; the four of them seemed to hit it off and had regular meetings at each other's homes, barbecues in the summer, evenings going to gigs and dances, and even the odd weekend away; life was starting to be good once again and things were getting better with Jack. She also met up with another couple of friends once a week and would catch up on the gossip and tell them about meeting up with her old school friend.

She was passing one day and decided to go and call on her friend. They had not arranged a meeting; when the door opened, it was her husband who said his wife had gone away to her parents for a few days, but said, "Come in anyway and have a coffee."

They chatted and he asked if she wanted to stay for some lunch, she said yes, they were joking with each other and she started talking in her flirty ways and one thing led to another, and they ended up in bed. This was the start of the affair; he would come to her house when Jack had gone to work, or they would take their own cars and meet up in a country lane, this went on for months and behind the deceit, they would still meet up as a foursome as if everything was normal.

She would meet up with her other friends and felt the need to load about her affair, but swore them to secrecy saying, "Don't say anything to anyone." Her friends tried to warn her she was playing with danger, and what would she do if Jack came home and caught them. She told them she was not bothered as once again, she was bored with her marriage and she did things with this man she had never done with her husband, he brought back the thrill again and he wanted her to leave Jack and go to South Africa with him, he had made up his mind he was going to leave his wife and two young daughters.

She told them she was nearly caught out one day when her parents came round and saw him coming down the stairs doing up his trousers, she got around it by saying he had called to see if she would like to go swimming with him and his daughters.

Her parents felt something was going on and questioned her but she denied everything.

He kept asking her to go away with him, but her parents were getting on in years and were now needing her help, and although her elder son had left home to live with his girlfriend, and the younger one also had a girlfriend, she felt she could not go with him. So reluctantly they said their goodbyes.

It hit her hard when he left, she missed him. She kept in touch with his wife as he had left her the house, she was distraught as she had not known he had been having an affair, and did not know who the other woman was but now she had to find work to continue to pay the mortgage.

Elisa was getting more and more depressed as she really would have liked to have gone with him, she arranged to see her doctor and confided in him about her affair and how it had left her, he then put her on anti-depressants.

Jack was caught up with his work and thought she was suffering because of the break-up, and with the friendship, and even said he did not see that coming and thought they seemed a happy couple and certainly did not tell him he was playing around.

Her elder son had heard rumours about his mum and questioned her as he was not happy seeing the situation between his mum and his dad. But once again, she strongly denied anything was going on and she and his dad were alright.

He told his parents that he wanted to go to Australia as a friend had gone out there and was doing well found work and was enjoying life. He applied and was accepted and as soon as his visa came through, the family gave him a farewell party and he went to start a new life.

Her younger son also had a girlfriend and spent a lot of time at her place, which left her and Jack with their own company; again she was getting bored as Jack did not want to go out in the evenings as he came home from work feeling very tired and lots of headaches, he would not even consider a holiday when she mentioned it to him did not want to go away.

Elisa's parents were now needing more help as her mother had developed dementia and her father had mobility problems and had to give up driving so her days were being filled by cleaning and shopping for them. And now having just one day to meet up with her few friends.

Elisa tried to fill her days by going on bike rides, walking her dog, and joining a few clubs which would mean she could snatch a day trip now and again with the ladies in the clubs.

To her, life became mundane, the same routine day after day even her friends when she met up noticed the change in her and how withdrawn she had become, and she had nothing to brag about.

She needed sex; she needed relief and there was no one to satisfy her needs; her body was throbbing.

She was on her own at home reminiscing thinking of the days with Bob all those years ago, she suddenly felt as if he was near and could smell his familiar aftershave, her thoughts were taking her back to how he made her feel and she could feel herself getting aroused, but had no one to satisfy her, she then rummaged through her drawer and found her vibrator, she was thinking she needed this now, she took off her clothes and stood looking at her still slim body in the mirror and imagined Bob coming up behind her and caressing her breasts; she was ready to insert the vibrator, into her throbbing vagina, when she switched on, the disaster, the battery was flat, she wanted it now but had to look for some batteries, could find none to fit and in desperation took the ones out from the doorbell. They worked and she managed to get it going and was experiencing sheer bliss and screaming out to Bob, "Why did you have to leave me we were good together?"

She was thankful she was in the house alone as she was feeling out of this world with the power of the vibrator, she reached her climax. And finally felt sexually relieved.

She knew things were stale with her husband and did not want to be in the home with him, so made many excuses to go out, either dog-walking or going to see her sister or a friend, but was longing to find herself a new lover.

She started to walk the dog about three times a day usually over the old airfield where she met up with other dog owners and would let the dogs have a run-around while they had a chat.

One morning, she decided to do an early run, it was a nice sunny morning and she got there before the others arrived having the walk to herself, she suddenly felt the call of nature and had to relieve herself, she tied her dog to a tree and went behind a bush, as she was coming out and straightening herself, she heard a man's voice talking to her dog, he turned as she approached and said, "Oh, hello I thought this little dog here tied up had been abandoned."

Elisa turned on the charm and in her flirty way said, "Whoops, call of nature," and she laughed, "I have been caught out."

As she looked at him, she felt as if an electric shock had gone through her as she sized this man up.

He was not that good-looking and was covered in tattoos, but she felt a magnetism toward him, and there would have been a difference in their ages; he was a lot younger. They seemed to bounce off each other with the chat he had a good sense of humour and as they carried on walking, she felt she had known him for years.

When the walk came to an end, he told her he worked shifts but would like to meet up again to which she readily agreed.

She went on her daily walks with the hope of seeing him again but did not see anything of the man, and was thinking *Oh, well just a chance meeting it was not to be.*

When she turned and heard, "Hi, Elisa, it's me not been around recently due to work, how have you been?" Her smile broadened and her heart did a double somersault as she saw who it was and the cheeky banter started between them. The hour walk went by so quickly and she knew she wanted to see more of this man.

She had started to see a couple of new friends who she met up with once a week and could not wait to tell them all about the meeting her new encounter, and would ask them to promise her that they would not tell Jack, she would tell them she was not happy at home and wanted to get away, but could not afford to leave.

The next time she met her man-friend, she told him she was unhappy at home, he told her he had two daughters but did not live with their mother and it was an on-and-off relationship with her. She started to cry and with that, he put his arms around her and started to kiss her, he started to fondle her breasts; Elisa could feel the excitement rising in her, and next thing, they had secured the dogs and slipped out of sight behind the bushes, she was grabbing at him and pulling at his trousers, and he was pulling down her leggings and pushed her to the ground and entered her. When it was over, she felt no signs of guilt for again cheating on Jack, just knew she wanted more from this man.

She met up with him as often as she could when dog-walking; her sister went on holiday and she said she would check the house, which gave her ample opportunity to meet the tattoo man at her house for more sex.

When she had her next outing with her girlfriends, she could not wait to inform them about how good sex was with this new man, she would go past his home when walking her dog in the hope of seeing him, but he would never invite her inside in case his daughters saw her and told their mother. But one day they did see her flirting with their dad, and walking the dogs holding hands, the girls questioned their dad as to what was going on.

After they saw the two of them together, Elisa started to get threats from them telling her to back off and leave their dad alone or she would face a lot of trouble from them, they said they knew where she lived and would tell her husband, they called her an old slag and even started to put a thing on social media about her.

When she told her friends about it, they said, "We did warn you to be careful," but all she said was she was not doing anything wrong; they were just enjoying each other's company, and she was not breaking up a marriage, as he was not married to the woman and they were both adults just having a bit of fun.

The thing was she did not realise at first that her son had heard things and had also seen on social media the threats being made, put two and two together and realised it was his mum they were talking about. He approached her on it but as usual, she denied it.

Things at home were not wonderful, Jack was always tired and very irritable and they were always arguing he was having constant headaches and she kept trying to get him to go to see the doctor, but Jack kept putting it off, he kept saying it was because of his eyes, he was having problems with pressure in the eyes and having injections and thought that was contributing to the headaches when one morning he was standing in front of her talking, but his eyes were not looking directly at her, she commented to him that was not right and she would make him an appointment at the doctor.

On the same day of the appointment, it was her mother's birthday, and she was now in a nursing home, so she was working between looking after her father who lived alone in the bungalow and visiting her mum; they had arranged with the staff to do a birthday party and her brothers and sisters and family would come and Jack after he had been to the doctor.

They all went ahead to the home and the time was getting on and no sign of Jack, when her phone started ringing, it was Jack and he was at the hospital and could she come along. She and her son arrived and were directed to the waiting room, then called in where Jack was sitting with the doctor looking shocked, he looked at them both and brought his hand across his throat and said, "I am fucked."

She said, "What are you talking about?" The doctor told them both to sit down and then explained that Jack had a brain tumour. Her son turned to her with a look of hate and whispered, "It's all your fault."

They left the hospital in shock and with more follow-up appointments for Jack. During the time they were waiting for appointments to come through, Jack was suffering horrendous pain and an ambulance had to come; they did not think he would make it, and because no will had been made, they had to get a solicitor to go to the hospital, he was in a good number of weeks, having treatment as they said the brain tumour was un operable, and it was just an amount of time. He underwent chemo and radiography treatment, was given a mass of medication, and started to improve but could no longer work as the diagnosis was terminal.

Her son blamed her for her playing around and said his dad should know what had been happening, and the daughters of her lover were also threatening they would do things to her, they knew where she lived.

She was so concerned because her son had insisted that she bring Jack over to his flat to talk things out, and she really thought she had blown it this time and was about to lose everything.

She managed to convince them nothing had been going on and this man was just a dog-walking friend and they all met up together.

Jack had known about an affair in the past and he made her swear to him while he was alive that she promised she would not go with another man, and this she did.

Living with the Tumour

Jack suffered many mood swings and was in constant pain in his head even with the strong medication he was given did not always help. Elisa became very frustrated as she did not know what to do to help him; she did attend the hospital visits to the consultant who explained to her about the tumour that they could not remove it and how it was likely to affect Jack. The consultant explained how it could affect his sexual libido, but could give him some medication to help, Jack declined that and Elisa said, "Don't worry, we will be ok."

Elisa told her friends about the visit to the hospital and told them what the doctor had said about their sex life, but said to her friends they were still able to do it which kept Jack satisfied but she lacked the excitement, but also told them she had made a promise to Jack that as long as he lived, it would be only him.

Three years went by and Jack was still around and surprisingly coping quite well. He still attended his hospital visits, but when they suggested having a scan, he would decline as he said it would worry him more if he was told it was getting larger and was starting to grow again, he would rather not know as he knew there would be nothing at all they could do, so he just plodded on in his daily routine.

Winter went into spring and Elisa felt life was just run of the mill.

One day she was out shopping at her local supermarket; when she had finished, she was on her way to her car, when her bag split and her shopping went all over the place, a man stopped to help her when she looked up she said, "Thank you," then said, "I know you. Weren't you at my school and my sister fancied the pants off you?"

He then started to laugh and said, "You look familiar. Who is your sister?" She gave her name and said she herself was a year younger. He then asked if she was married and she told him what was happening in her life. He then told her that he was divorced and had just bought a flat which overlooked a park, and in further discussion found it was the park where she sometimes walks her dog.

He then said, "We must keep in touch and I will look out for you when you come to the park with your dog," and with that, they exchanged telephone numbers and said goodbye.

A week later, it was a warm sunny day so she decided to go to the park, she told Jack where she was going and if would he like to come along but he said he was tired and would stay at home.

She did not phone to say she was coming, but as she was walking along, she heard a male voice shout "Hi, I am over here," She turned and saw him sitting on a bench, hot and cold shivers ran over her she thought how sexy and tanned he looked sitting there. She let the dog off the leash so it could have a run-around and went over to sit by him, she found him easy to talk to and he had the same flirty manner that she had, they seemed to have quite a lot in common, he liked cycling, one of her hobbies and swimming, he told her he had been decorating his flat but was trying to get used to being on his own and felt quite lonely at times. Elisa looked at her watch and didn't realise the time, and said she had better make a move and get back home, she called her dog and said, "Goodbye, hope to see you next time I come out here."

A few weeks later when she arrived at the park, it was drizzling with rain and she did not expect to see him, but once again, he was sitting on the same bench which backed onto the garden of his flat.

The rain started to get heavy and she said, "I had better go," when he said, "Why don't you come into the flat and have a coffee and I can show you around?"

Elisa did not want to rush back home so she said, "Ok, that would be nice." She felt so relaxed with him.

This was the start; he showed her around the flat, "This is the lounge newly decorated." She commented on what a good job he had done and liked his choice of décor. Then he said laughingly, "This is my lonely bedroom."

Elisa took the bait and laughing said, "We will have to make it not so lonely," and with that, he grabbed her and kissed her, then he pulled away saying, "No, I can't do this to him," and with that, Elisa turned and left the flat.

A Letter from Ireland

Elisa was feeling rejected after her meeting at the park, and she was sitting wondering what to do next as she knew she wanted to see him again.

There was a sudden banging on her door which brought her back to reality; when she opened the door, the postman nearly threw the package at her, she looked at the name and address thinking *I hadn't ordered anything*. Jack was in the lounge and shouted who was it. She replied saying, "It is ok; it's only a small package for me."

She went back into the kitchen and opened it to find an envelope sealed with her name and address on it and a letter from Cathy's mother; as she read the letter the colour drained from her and she felt she was near to fainting, Cathy's mother was broken-hearted to convey to Elisa that Cathy had died; she had taken an overdose as she could cope no longer. Since moving to Ireland in the beginning, she started to improve, and then her health took a turn for the worse. She could not cope with her son as he reminded her of the way she had been used and cheated on and the loss of her home. She had been taken to hospital for a few months and it seemed she was starting to get better and was allowed home for weekends, but one weekend, they went into her bedroom and found her.

Although they were getting on in years, they were managing to look after the children. She was sorting through her things and found this envelope addressed to Elisa.

Elisa pulled herself together and thought *I can't open that envelope yet*, so she went to her room and hid it till later when Jack was going out to see his friend; she then went into the lounge and was sobbing and through her tears told Jack what had happened to Cathy. He then came up to her and put his arms around her. *Dear Jack*, she thought, *even with your brain tumour you have the heart to comfort me*; they talked briefly of the time when they were neighbours and good friends, and how sad it was that Cathy took her life.

That evening when Jack went out to meet his friend for a few hours, he said he would not be too late, so she settled down with a glass of wine and to watch a film, when she had a sudden thought about the envelope and went to fetch it; she looked at the writing but did not recognise the writing; it was not Cathy's or her mother's; she opened it to find a copy of the DNA letter and she started to panic and was shaking. How did that get to Cathy but it definitely had not been opened, so Cathy could not have seen it, and in big scrawly letters was a note saying, 'I have the original papers,' but again she did not recognise the writing.

There was nothing to imply in the letter from Cathy's mother that Cathy knew anything about the DNA test, and that her son was Bob's child.

With shaking hands, she carefully folded the form and went to find a secure place to hide it.

When Jack came home, he found her sleeping on the sofa, TV on and an empty bottle of wine, he started to wake her up and she was saying, "It's bad, it's bad the letter." But Jack just assumed she had too much to drink and was upset about Cathy; he was thinking in the morning she would have a pretty thick head.

The next day, he was right; she had a bad head not only from the wine but also the worry of what was going to happen next. Who was that person? Would they write again or even turn up?

Rejected

It was not only the letter that was worrying Elisa but her thoughts were also returning to her man-friend in the park; she had never felt so rejected when he said to her, "I can't do this to Jack."

Elisa met up with her friends and told them what had happened and also said no man had turned her down before and started to laugh; her friends were getting tired of hearing the things she was doing as they felt sorry for Jack who was innocent to all of this and still thought the world of her, but she would relish going into detail of the other affairs as if she gained excitement reliving them, but she had no conscience or guilt of what she was doing behind Jack's back.

She would invite her friends to the house where they met Jack but they felt guilty trying to talk to him knowing what Elisa was up to and he being so ill.

She was crafty, she thought, bringing her friends to the house Jack could see who she was meeting and it was a good cover for her when she wanted to meet her male friend.

She knew she could not let things end before they had started; she wanted him and next time, she would not be rejected.

Weeks went by; winter was drawing in; the weather was not good for taking the dog to the park. She had the man's telephone number but would not ring or text should Jack pick up her phone and question who he was.

Jack was in a lot of pain and the medication would not always agree with him; there were days when his temper made him aggressive and irritable; these times he would go off on his own, those times did worry Elisa and she felt she had to get away also out of her home.

Jack always enjoyed his motorbike and would go off for a ride to cool down, but lately, his eyesight had got worse and he was told not to ride the bike. He was lonely and missed the company of his workmates and took out his frustrations on Elisa.

She tried to get him to agree to go on a short weekend away with her, thought a change would do him good, but he did not want to go; she was beginning to feel like a prisoner in her own home; the dark nights meant she could not go out far when walking the dog; she could not go for a bike ride, or even see her friends as they were tied up with their own families.

She started to spend more time on the computer chatting with people she had never met. There was an older gentleman who she found was on his own and lived locally, so she arranged to meet him for a coffee after she had finished her shopping and ended up pouring out her heart to him about Jack and his illness. He was a good listener and she found they had a lot in common despite their ages, he also enjoyed bike rides out to the country he enjoyed walking and found he liked to go swimming so they arranged to meet up at the local swimming pool.

They met up a few times; she enjoyed his company but that was as far as it was going to go; she even arranged for him to come and meet Jack thinking it would be company for him another man to talk to.

But she did not tell Jack she thought he had a crush on her, as he had bought her expensive perfume and chocolates and flowers. She felt he wanted more from her but told him it was only friendship and she did not fancy him but could still come to the house to visit her and Jack. She started to make excuses that she had appointments to go to when she knew he was coming.

She was now getting no sex from Jack, because of his pain and he was so restless that she had decided it would be better for her to sleep in the spare room.

Their son who had gone to Australia kept in touch by video link; he now had a partner and a child, their first grandson; he could not afford to travel back home when he heard about his father's illness, but asked if they would like to come over and stay for a holiday and meet the child.

Jack spoke to his doctor who said it would not be advisable for him to travel such a long journey and the pressure, but Jack suggested that Elisa go over on her own for a few weeks, and said he would be alright and he could look after the dog and if he needed any help, the younger son and partner could come and stay.

Australia

It was coming up to Christmas when a flight was arranged for Elisa to go and see her son. Jack seemed happy to be on his own. Elisa had prepared meals and put them in the freezer so he did not have to worry about food and just pop it into the microwave.

Arrangements had been made with the younger son to check his dad was alright and that they would stay at the weekends as Elisa was going to stay in Australia for four weeks.

When she arrived in Australia, there was no one to meet her at the airport; she phoned her son who had been caught up in traffic but eventually arrived and took her back on a long journey to his place in the bush. His place was very basic not what she was expecting at all and her first impression of his partner left a lot to be desired and she felt friction. His partner worked at the hospital quite a distance from home and arrangements were made that he stayed at home to look after the child while she was at work; she also found out that she had rejected the child not long after birth and her son had stepped in to look after the child and it was evident the child did not connect with his mother; during her stay she made quite a bond with the little fellow.

Her son said he had an appointment in Sydney which meant he would be away for the day and his partner would also be at work, so she was left to look after her grandson.

It was a very hot summer and even the air conditioning did not cool her, so while she was in the house on her own, she just wore her bra and pants, she had been playing with the little one to tire him out, fed him and put him down for a rest, was just about to fetch a cool drink for herself and to settle to sunbathe when she heard a knock at the door, she grabbed her sarong to cover herself and opened the door to find a man just staring at her.

She sized him up and down and was pleasantly surprised; he was tall well built with a golden tan and bushy hair; he looked not much older than her son, thinking he could be a friend, she put a smile on her face and said, "What can I do for you?" The man answered in broad Australian that he was a neighbour and her son's land backed onto his and that the fencing had been vandalised and his animals had strayed over and caused some damage, but he had got them back and had repaired the fence.

Elisa was smiling and saying thank you and that her son would be grateful and she invited him in for a drink not realising that this was the neighbour her son had a lot of problems with.

She offered him the drink but he grabbed her hand; she felt like an electric shock had shot through her body; she had no man touch her for months; he said he had been watching her since she arrived; he could see her when she was in the garden in her bikini and could not believe she was his neighbour's mother.

She sensed he was breathing heavily as he looked her up and down and could see her bra and pants beneath the sarong. Elisa did not feel frightened; she felt excited and wanted this man, as she turned to get her drink, he stepped out to stop her and pulled off her sarong leaving her standing in her bra and pants; she stooped to pick it up and he lunged at her his hands around her breasts; she grabbed at his shorts pulling them down to expose his extended penis; he looked surprised that she did not resist then pulled off her bra and pants pushing his penis between her legs; he then pulled her to the floor inserted his penis and frantically took her.

Elisa held on to him crying out, "Give it to me."

The only thing that stopped her and she broke away was when she heard her grandson crying out.

The man got up, put on his shorts and said, "I will be back," and then he left. Elisa put on her underwear and the sarong and went to see the child, and was thinking about what had just happened with a stranger, but she felt exhilarated; she had not had sex that good for such a long time and hoped she would see him again before she went back home to England.

When her son and partner arrived home, she had a meal ready for them and assured them the little fellow had been good and she had been alright but she was thinking about the neighbour and felt it would be better not to say anything about him coming to the house as she thought the fence had been repaired so there was no need to say anything, but she was hoping there would be a way of meeting up with him again and without arousing suspicions with her son.

Time was running out and she would soon be getting ready to go home. A few days later, her son said he would have to take his son for a hospital check-up and would be away most of the day would she like to come, but Elisa said she would stay at the house to relax and catch with some sun rays as she had heard it was very cold back home in England; her son accepted that, but in her head, she was making plans to see if she could meet up again with that young man.

After her son left, she showered, put on her bikini and shorts and went for a walk to the top field it was so quiet, no one was around; even the animals had been moved to another field. She was so hot and started to make her way back when she saw an old barn, so for a bit of shade, she decided to go in there.

She was just stepping inside when she felt a rough hold on her shoulders and she was thrown to the ground; this she did not expect and was trying to focus in the dark who was standing there as they did not speak. This she did not expect; the man was ripping off her clothes, then standing astride her, she started shouting, "Who is it? Who are you?" With that, he grabbed at her breasts all she could hear was his heavy breathing and then pulled her legs apart and pushed his head in her vagina rubbing up and down; she grabbed at his hair and felt the thick fuzzy hair and then knew it was the neighbour. He went astride her and pushed his penis into her mouth saying, "Suck it, you bitch." Elisa was not frightened; she was exhilarated enjoying this sexual experience; she gave him what he wanted, and he was shouting in ecstasy, she then said, "Come into me, give it to me," which he did, then rolled off totally exhausted. He lay there saying nothing not touching her, then grunting got up and left the barn.

She got up to find her clothes, she felt as if her body had been battered but had no regrets as she enjoyed the violent sex.

She went to the barn door, her eyes now became accustomed to the light; there was no sign of the man; he had disappeared.

She made her way back home; her hair was all over the place, her clothes were dirty and ripped, and she needed to get back home and have a shower before her son returned.

Two days later, it was time for her to return home, her son took her to the airport and said their goodbyes.

Returning Home

Days after returning home, she found that Jack had coped well looking after the dog and himself; the younger son and partner had made frequent visits to check and clean the house for him; there was one incident where he was in a lot of pain and needed to see the doctor, but told them not to inform Elisa as he did not want her to cut her holiday short.

Jack was still not interested in going out but wanted to hear all the news about his son and grandson and how he was getting on.

Elisa did not elaborate too much on their son's relationship but said he thought the world of his son and spent as much time as possible with him.

Elisa had a flashback to the neighbour and of their first encounter, the thought sent excitement through her; then she thought about the last meeting and how he had treated her, she thought was it because he did not get on with her son and took a form of sexual revenge on his mother. But little did he know just how much she had enjoyed that encounter.

She was brought back to reality hearing her mobile phone ringing, thinking it was one of her friends wanting to catch up on the news of her holiday, with shock, she heard her son in Australia shouting at her calling her a slag. When he finally calmed down but was still angry, he said, "You thought you had got away with it?"

She said, "What are you talking about?"

"Drop the innocent act," he said, "you have been caught out after you left, I checked the security camera that I had set up to watch how my partner reacted with the child and found you having sex with the neighbour who has caused me a lot of trouble. This time you cannot deny it and I have sent a copy to my brother who also has proof. When he told me you had been having affairs, I did not want to believe him but now I do. Dad should know what you have been up to behind his back. You should be ashamed of yourself with him being so ill," and with that, he cut off the phone call leaving Elisa shocked and feeling physically sick to the stomach, *what was she going to do if they showed the video to Jack?*

She could not face Jack she had to think and calm herself, so shouted to him, "That was my friend on the phone; she wants me to go round to her house so see you later."

Jack unknown of what had just gone on said, "Ok, see you later."

When she came home, she did not know what to expect, *had her sons spoken to Jack? Was there going to be a big argument?* She was in a state of fear if Jack threw her out where would she go, she could not go to her friends as their husbands were friends with Jack and would hate Elisa knowing she had been having affairs when he was so ill.

All this was going on in her head when Jack came through from the kitchen and said, "I thought I would make a drink, do you want one?"

He was smiling and said, "Did you tell your friend all about your holiday in Australia?" She felt relief; her sons had not told him but was thinking about when would they tell him and when would the balloon go up. She tried to act normal and responded and said, "We caught up with everything and the girls want me to go on a day trip with them." She tried to make the conversation as normal as possible and not show her anxiety.

The phone started to ring and she jumped out of her skin, Jack noticed and said, "What's up with you? You're a bit jumpy," and he went to answer the phone. As she waited for him to come back into the room, he shouted, "It's the plumber I called him as I found a leak in the bathroom." Elisa breathed a sigh of relief but thought, I hope I am not going to be like this every time the phone rings.

The younger son could not bring himself to talk to her after he had seen the video from his brother but sent her a message saying, 'Be out when I come over with my daughter to see Dad, I don't want her associating with you. I will come and see my dad and I am sure with all of your lies, you can come up with something to explain why you are not there.'

He was coming home so Elisa had to think of something convincing to tell Jack so he would not get suspicious as she idolised her granddaughter and looked forward to seeing her.

Elisa could not use any of her friends to back her up as she had not told them about the video and how her boys had turned against her.

Before she went to Australia, she had talked to Jack about going on a retreat weekend she had enquired but was told were booked up, but had left her information should they have a cancellation.

She would use that as her excuse and say a weekend had become available, so she now had to find somewhere to stay;

she told Jack to explain to her granddaughter and also messaged her.

The granddaughter was getting older and now did not want to visit so often as she had her own friends she wanted to meet up with.

The younger son shared the same fishing interests as his dad and arranged fishing weekends away with him.

Elisa spent a lonely time in her room on her weekend away, and started to suffer from anxiety, living in fear, *will her sons tell their dad*?

Boredom was setting in, and because she had not met up with all her friends since coming home, and the few friends who she would normally confide in, she felt she could not tell them what had happened in Australia or about her son seeing the video of her with the neighbour he hated, and how he had passed it on to his brother and now both had disowned her.

She felt she had to find something to do with her time and thought about part-time work which would get her away from Jack for a few hours and try and get on with things the best she could.

Her relationship with Jack now felt like brother and sister; he many times seemed lost in a world of his own; he was having problems remembering things and was not happy to go out on his own so arrangements always had to be made that he was always with someone.

Elisa did notice that Jack was always happy to see his son and daughter-in-law, while she was in Australia, arrangements had been put in place to check on Jack and also to stay over at the weekend.

One weekend, his son could not come over as he had arranged to take his daughter camping with a club, so his wife said she would go and stay and tidy the place and make sure Jack was alright.

They decided they would have a takeaway and watch a film for the evening they had a few drinks and a fun-filled evening and went off to bed.

The next morning, Jack had slept in late, was just getting up to go to the bathroom and he met Sara on the landing; she was just coming out of the bathroom with the towel draped around her and bumped into Jack. As she turned, her towel got caught on the door handle and as she moved, it fell off her leaving her standing there naked. Jack just stood looking at her, and as she turned and looked up at him; she could see the look on his face that he wanted her; she stretched out her arm to pick up the towel and he took hold of her arm pulling him to her and started to kiss her lips, then her neck and down to her breasts, and before they knew it he had lifted her up and took her into the bedroom; she did not resist but clung on to him responding to his needs; he took her to places his son never had; when they had finished, she turned to him and said, "I do not feel guilty I am not sorry and don't you feel guilty either."

She was due to stay another night with him, and while there, Elisa made her phone call to Jack saying it wouldn't be long now before I was back home.

Jack turned to Sara and said, "I am going to feel so guilty as I have never been unfaithful to her." Sara could see his distress, but assured him he must not feel guilty, she said, "This was meant to be I wanted you and you wanted me." That night was even more blissful for both of them.

Elisa was oblivious to what had happened; Jack had seemed pleased and normal when she arrived back home and she had no idea of what had happened between him and her daughter-in-law.

She did feel a smugness with Sara that she had never felt before, but she also remembered she had told her about one of her affairs and had sworn her to secrecy, but she also felt her son must have told her about what had happened in Australia and the video. She also knew she could not approach her on the matter as she knew she would tell her son.

It was taking its toll trying to act happy in front of Jack, so she was relieved when she was able to get away for a few hours at her job working in a charity shop and able to talk to other people for a few hours. While she was there, she met a young woman who was pregnant; when they were chatting, she found out she was going through a similar situation; she did not know who the father of the child she was carrying was; her husband or the man she had a one night stand with, but he has found her and wanted more to do with her, she said she would have to do a DNA test when the baby was born.

This brought back memories to her and she thought, *I must check and see that paperwork of mine is still in the safe place when I get home.*

She arrived back to find Jack fast asleep in his chair and didn't hear her come in; she took off her coat and thought, *I will just go and check that paperwork and letter from Cathy's mother that she had put in a safe place in the secret drawer.*

She opened the drawer to find it was empty; panic started within her and her heart was racing; she pulled out all the drawers thinking it may have fallen down the back; she pulled all of her clothes out no sign of it. She heard a movement behind her and Jack was standing there saying, "I didn't hear you come in. What are you doing?" She could not tell him what it was she was looking for just said she had lost some special earrings and thought they might have got caught up in the clothes or fallen down the back of the drawers.

He seemed happy enough with her explanation and left her to carry on sorting the clothes and the drawers out.

Elisa felt so anxious that someone had been through her things while she had been away; *was it Jack but surely had it been him, he would have confronted her; was it her son but he had not said anything or was it Sara and she was biding her time to bring light to it, was she going to use it to blackmail her?*

Things Were Changing

Elisa felt she was treading on eggshells around Jack as he seemed to show no interest in her sexually since she had arrived back home from Australia; she accepted that he was having more and more bad days from the pain in his head from the tumour, and put things down to that. They were also now not sleeping together in the same room as Jack had suggested because he was so restless at night and also because of her back it would be better for them to have separate rooms so she could sleep downstairs she did not argue as she agreed with him it would be better for the both of them.

She did notice that when her daughter-in-law came over and saw they now slept in separate rooms, she gave a sly smug smile, she also saw how Jack was so happy to see her and how he perked up when she came over.

Sarah had been secretly having the occasional meetings with Jack when Elisa was not around when she went to see her friends and felt safe that she would not be back to interrupt them, and had also spent the weekend with Jack when Elisa went away on a weekend beauty course assuring her, she would look after Jack.

Elisa had not seen much of her younger son or even her granddaughter as she was now at the age she wanted to spend time with her friends, and when she did meet up with her younger son, things were very strained, yet Jack did not seem to notice.

One afternoon, Elisa was in the kitchen preparing a meal, when the door opened and in came a tear-stained Sara, Elisa went over to her and asked what was wrong, what was worrying her.

They sat down just the two of them as Jack had gone to sleep. Sara started crying and was saying things were not right with her husband and their relationship had not been right for some time and she felt it was leading up to a break-up.

Elisa tried to console her and said all marriages at some time tend to go through bad patches, she also knew that with her relationship with her son, she could not interfere or talk to him, but she said to Sara, "You know you can always come here for a break if things get to difficult."

Little did Elisa know or realise she was playing right into Sara's plans.

Elisa felt trapped within her own thoughts and felt she had no one to confide in; she no longer divulged things to her friends when they met up; they were more concerned about Jack's health and how he was coping.

She was sitting having her morning coffee, looked at her watch and thought it was a nice sunny day; she would escape for a while, so she told Jack she would take the car and take the dog off for a walk in the park; she asked if he would like to come along but he declined saying he had some woodwork to attend to. She had intended to drive to the park that had a pond as her dog liked to jump in and have a swim but her mind was wandering and she missed her turning, so she carried on to the other park where she had met her man-friend months before.

When she arrived, she found there were a lot of dog walkers around and a few people she had got to know from her walks before. Her mood started to lift as she got chatting and laughing with them; the dogs were running and chasing each other she felt this was like old times, then she heard a yelp and her dog was limping so she ran to see what had happened when she slipped and fell on the grass, as she was trying to get up she heard a familiar male voice said, "I thought it was you are you in trouble again." She looked up to see the man who had rejected her, as he helped her up she fell against his chest and her heart was racing as she felt his arms around her. She tried to compose herself by saying, "I think my dog has been hurt and I was running to see." She checked her dog's paw to find a thorn and was able to remove it and her dog then ran off to play again with the others leaving her alone with this man.

He smiled and said, "I have missed you and thought how rejected you must have felt at our last meeting. I come down most days with the hope that you would come back, I did not want to phone or text as I did not want to cause you any problems."

Elisa could hardly contain herself she felt herself bubbling up with excitement, he still wanted to see her.

She briefly explained she had been away on holiday to see her son and that was the reason she had not been here to walk her dog. She could not tell him she had felt totally rejected by him, she tried to keep the conversation going with him by telling him how Jack was, then she looked at her watch and said she had better make her way back home.

He took hold of her hand and said, "You will come back, won't you? I have missed your company."

Elisa could feel the excitement rising within her and heard herself say, "Oh yes, I will definitely be coming back."

In her mind, Elisa was feeling happier knowing there was someone who cared for her and she knew she would have to be careful and this time not to tell anyone this time. She also said to herself she must not come on too fast to him let him come to her in his own time let him make the first move.

She decided she would not rush back to the park and left her walks there for a couple of weeks. When she did eventually go, he was there sitting on the bench looking so forlorn all she wanted to do was run to him and give him a hug, but she walked along casually with her dog and shouted, "Hi, are you ok? Long time no see." Her heart was beating frantically as all she wanted to do was kiss him.

He shouted over to her, "I thought you were not going to come back, come over here and sit down so we can have a chat." She went over and as she sat by him she could feel him trembling, she took hold of his hand and asked if he was alright, and to her it felt like a bolt of lightning, shooting through her just to touch him; he then drew her into his arms and said, "Thank God, I thought I had lost you." She cupped his face and saw fear in his eyes, she reassured him and told him, "You have got me as long as you want me."

He told her he still felt guilty because of Jack, but he wanted her; he needed her. The time with him went fast and she said she had better get back home with the dog, but she would arrange for a time they could be together; reluctantly he let her go.

When she walked through to the kitchen to wipe down the dog and give him his meal, she could hear Jack laughing, at first, she thought they had got visitors but when she went into the lounge, he turned and the smile left his face and accusingly asked, "Where have you been? You have been a long time." She explained she had been to the park and had met up with other dog walkers she had not seen for a long time, and they had a coffee in the park and a chat catching up and did not realise the time, she added you could have come along and you would have met them.

He answered by saying he was getting concerned, and that Sara had called in and brought some cake, and spent an hour with him. She just said, "Oh, that was nice." She had not told him about their conversation and the problem between her and their son, she thought it was better not to say anything, and obviously, Sara had not told Jack anything; he just was happy he had some company; she certainly brought a smile to his face; he also added that Sara had said, "If you have to go on any more courses, she will come and keep me company, if their son can't manage it because he has accepted more overtime at work."

Elisa thought this could not have worked out better as she could now make an excuse to see and stay over with her new man-friend, she could not wait to see and tell him the news.

The next day, she said to Jack, "I am taking the dog again to the park. It may be a while if the others turn up and we have a coffee and natter again. Do you want to come?"

Jack shouted, "No, I don't feel too good today so I will stay here, will see you later."

When she arrived, her friend was not there in the usual meeting place, so she let her dog off lead to run with the others and went to meet up with the others for a chat which also gave her an alibi if anything came out. She was about to go when she heard her name being called, it was him he was running towards her and saying, "I am so sorry I could not get here as I was helping a neighbour who had a fall."

She grabbed hold of his hand and said, "Let's sit down. I have some news to tell you." He was looking worried was she going to say she did not want to see him anymore, but she smiled and said, "Let me put you in the picture," and explained how she now had a way that they could meet up and be together, she would arrange a weekend in the next few weeks.

He said to her, "So that you are not seen coming to my place, let us arrange a weekend away."

Elisa went home feeling so happy, and that evening scrolled through her computer to find dates and places of courses to show Jack, but also to make arrangements to meet her new man.

Jack encouraged her to go ahead and book because it would leave him free to see Sara.

The Threat

Elisa always had a close relationship with her granddaughter, but as she was growing up and making friends her own age, she did not see much of her, and also because of the situation with her son, they did not spend so much time together. She would keep in contact by texting and both would end up saying love and miss you. Elisa was scrolling through her emails. One morning when she was sitting having a coffee and came over a message supposedly from her granddaughter, she was very shocked by the way she approached her and was demanding she gave her £1000 and finished off the text by saying, 'I know what you have done and I have got proof'; it was an abrupt ending no love you and no explanation. Elisa could not believe this threatening message was from her granddaughter; she was shaking and in turmoil did she know something, had she found the missing paperwork, this was so not like her granddaughter.

She knew she would have to be careful; she could not tell Jack she was asking for money and she would have to bide her time and tread carefully she could not believe her lovely granddaughter would try to blackmail her.

She was thinking had she overheard a conversation between her parents discussing what had happened in

Australia; she thought she would not respond to the email maybe someone else had got hold of her granddaughter's phone; no she would wait till the next time she came over to visit and try and approach things with her to see if she knows anything.

Suddenly she was brought back to reality when she heard Jack calling her name; she shut down her phone and went to see what was happening.

She was greeted with, "Have you sorted out that course you wanted to go on yet?" She thought it strange he should ask as usually she just told him when she had booked it. He then said, "I thought this course was important to you and you had to sign up, and didn't you say you would have to stay over three nights?"

She said, "Yes, I was going to arrange it today but I wanted to check that you would be alright while I am away." Jack said he had been talking to Sara and she said she and the family would make arrangements to come and stay if he needed them and he told her that he did not need them all to come, so Sara said she would come if needed and that's how we left things.

Elisa still had that nauseating feeling about the email but decided to go ahead and book the course which was in a week's time.

She would have to get in touch with her man-friend and tell him the news and for him to arrange to go with her. Later that afternoon, she told Jack she would take the dog to the park and would he like to come and meet the other dog walkers but he said no he would stay at home.

When she arrived there, her man-friend was sitting on the bench talking to the others. She let her dog off the lead to run and play with the other dogs and then went to say hello to the group; she was hoping they would disperse so she could get the chance to talk to him on her own and tell him her news.

Eventually, it was just the two of them, she grabbed hold of his hand sending an electric shock through her body just touching him, she thought, *Oh God, I so want this man*. She told him what she had arranged and hoped he would be able to come. He put his arm around her and said, "I cannot wait." She said she would come to the park the next day and finalise their plans so that no one would see them going off together.

Later when she arrived back home, she heard voices; it was Sara and her granddaughter, they were laughing and joking with Jack. Her heart was racing, but she must keep calm and act natural. She shouted, "Hi, it's been a long while since I've seen you," directed to her granddaughter, who suddenly got up came over and gave her a hug. She looked into her eyes but could see no threatening look coming from her, surely it was not her who had sent that email to her.

She asked her what had she been up to, thought put the ball in her court, but she just said she had been busy with exams and then catching up with her friends.

Then Sara piped up, "Jack tells me you have arranged to go on another course and I have told him I can come over if he needs anything done."

Elisa thanked her saying, "I know you will look after him." She looked up and saw Sara's piercing eyes on her. She said, "Jack insisted I book and go on this course."

Sara suddenly snapped back saying, "We have been discussing things and I have said, I will be here if he needs me."

Elisa thought Sara was watching her, but why she knew about her marriage problems but she had not told Jack what was going on with her and their son. But she had the feeling something was not quite right.

As the pre-arranged weekend approached, it was hard for Elisa to contain her excitement; she told Jack this was a special course that would enhance her in many ways. Little did she know it was going to be the same for him with Sara.

The Weekend

Elisa said goodbye to Jack and told him if he needed her, she would be at the end of the phone. Jack reassured her he would be alright.

Little did she know he could not wait for her to go so that he could be with Sara; he knew she would look after him in more ways than one and the thought was exciting to him.

Elisa had no more emails from her granddaughter, and she was so looking forward to getting to know her new man.

They had arranged to meet at the station, but to sit apart, and to make out they did not know each other.

When they arrived in London, they then both went to the hotel together and checked in, went straight to the room; as they closed the door, they turned and went straight at each other frantically pulling off their clothes till they were naked.

Elisa's hands were frantically all over him, he was kissing her lips, her breasts and down to her vagina. Elisa was moaning from pure ecstasy, he also could not get enough, he pushed her onto the bed and pulled open her legs wide and started sucking her vagina; she was grabbing his head and pulling him up and pleading with him to enter her, it had been such a long time since he had been with a woman sexually; he could not believe how she had brought him to climax three times, and still did not want to stop.

Elisa could not believe how wonderful and tender this man was with her and wanted him more and more, did not want it to stop.

They had been in bed for hours; he looked towards the clock and said, "We had better get ready or we will miss our evening meal." He was reluctant to move but was thinking, *I have got three days of this, have I died and gone to heaven?*

The next morning, Elisa said she would have to show up at the course so she could prove to Jack that she had attended, she was hoping the day would go by quickly so that she could get back to the hotel, to resume their lovemaking.

When she arrived back at the hotel, she found he had arranged a table in the room with food and wine, she smiled and said that looked good but he looked even better and she was ravenous for him. She went closer and could smell his aftershave; he looked so handsome standing there with a glass of champagne for them both.

She slipped off her coat and just stood for a moment looking at him; he put down the glasses pulled her to him kissed her and then unzipped the front of her dress and started to fondle her breasts. Elisa's excitement was rising; she started to pull at his clothes to unzip his trousers, and her hand went inside to hold on to his penis; he was breathing heavily and opened up the zip further on her dress that fell to the floor leaving her naked; she fell to her knees pulling off his trousers and rubbing his penis all over her body and up to her mouth, he was groaning and his body was writhing; he came on to the floor pushed her legs apart and entered her bringing her sheer bliss and he at the same time. There was no thought of Jack on her mind or feeling of guilt; she was with this man and savouring every moment of him bringing her to a multitude climax.

Elisa was brought back to reality by her phone ringing and said she had better answer in case it was Jack.

She looked at the phone and said it was a number she did not recognise, but then said, "Hello, who is it?"

The voice that came back was that of her granddaughter saying, "Hi Nan, just checking you are ok enjoying the course and this is my new number had to get another phone as I lost the other one a few days ago."

Elisa told her she was fine and the course was intensive and now she was catching up on the theory homework, then said, "I will see you soon." She put down the phone and thought it could not have been her who sent the email, someone else must have got hold of her phone, was it her son or was it Sara?

When she went back to her man-friend; he could sense she was worried over something and asked if it was Jack and if he was alright and said if it was anything serious, she would have to go back. She could not tell him what it was just that it was not Jack.

In the meantime, no sooner had Elisa left the house, Sara arrived on her own much to Jack's relief. He had been excited at the thought of her coming to stay, he had a meal laid out with flowers and wine and just in case they had all arrived he was ready to say it was a thank-you for the help they had given him.

He was not going to rush anything, he wanted Sara to come to him when she was ready, so that evening they watched a film which got them both laughing and had a few drinks; the evening went by quickly they were both relaxed and Jack said, "I think it's time for bed, Sara," She was off to bed and would see him in the morning, Jack went off feeling a little dejected after what had happened before between them.

Jack lay in his bed unable to sleep knowing she was in the next room; he was restless when in the darkness he heard a door open and thought it was Sara going to the bathroom, but no, it was his door that had opened and he could see her naked silhouette standing in the doorway; he held out his arms to her and she came to him. He kissed her breasts sending a tingling through his body then pulled her onto the bed. She took hold of his penis and went astride him entering into her, and was frantically riding him and brought him to a climax quicker than she had expected; she then flopped to the side of him and held onto him thinking, *maybe this is enough for him tonight, but I still have two more nights.*

Disappointed

Elisa was preparing herself for her last day on the course, and one more wonderful night with this fantastic man. She went over and kissed him and said, "Usually, on the last day, we finish early so I will text you and we can maybe go out somewhere, then come back and celebrate our last night together, hope it will not be too long before I can sort something else out."

He said, "Ok, will see you later."

That morning at the course seemed to go on forever, and then there was the presentation of the diplomas, which she needed to show to Jack.

She looked at her watch; it was approaching 2'oclock when she was able to get away, she went to get her coat and got her phone out to text her man-friend to let him know she was on her way back, and saw she had a message from him saying he was sorry but he had a call from home and had to get back as there was an emergency; he had settled up at the hotel so she could make her way home and he would be in touch.

Elisa was in a panic, wondering what had happened and did not want to stay another night at the hotel on her own so she decided to make her way back home.

When she walked into her home, she saw Sara standing in her dressing gown, with a look of shock on her face and said, "We did not expect you back till tomorrow."

Elisa innocently said to her, "Are you ok? A bit early for your dressing gown on," to which Sara replied, "I have had a stomach upset and spent the day in bed, Jack has been looking after me."

Elisa said, "Oh, ok hope you are feeling a bit better. Where is Jack?" Sara replied saying Jack went to the chemist for something for her and the corner shop for a few things. With that, Jack walked through the door; he was shocked to see Elisa and said, "Is everything alright?"

She said, "The course finished early and I could see no point in staying an extra night so I came back home." She did not notice the bag he was holding that contained a bottle of wine and chocolates.

Sara had gone up to her room and got changed, she went quickly into Jack's room to make sure there was nothing of hers lying around.

When she came back down, Elisa said, "You don't have to go stay and have something to eat," but Sara said she still felt a bit rough and did not want to pass anything on to them so she would make my way back home and have a quiet night to herself till the others came home.

Jack went up to her, gave her a hug and said, "Thank You, hope you feel better soon," gave her a wink and she left.

Jack spoke to Elisa about her course and said he had missed her, and when he was out, he had bought a bottle of wine and chocolates for her homecoming which should have been the next day, she thanked him and said what a lovely thought, but she felt she needed an early night as all the studying for the course had made her rather tired.

Jack had accepted that and felt quite relieved when she went to her room; she thought she would text her man-friend to let him know she had got back and hoped all was ok with him and she hoped to come to the park the next day with the dog and to find out why he had to rush back.

The next morning, she and Jack chatted over breakfast, discussing how Sara was and that she would give her a call later; she then did some work around the home then said to Jack she would take the dog for a run to the park as she thought he would have missed his run off the lead with the other dogs, once again she said would you like to come along, but was relieved when he said no.

She arrived at the park chatted to the other dog walkers let her dog off to have a run-around and made her way over to their meeting place, she waited for a while but he did not arrive.

She took out her phone and tried to phone but the operator's voice said the number was unobtainable; she thought maybe she had rung the wrong number and tried again, it came up with the same thing, so she tried to text and it came up failure.

She was very concerned now, but time was getting on and she had told Jack she would not be long, so she called the dog and made her way back home.

Elisa came into the kitchen and sat chatting to Jack for a while saying she felt sad as she had just heard a dog walker friend had been rushed into hospital, the lady had no family so a neighbour for the time being was looking after her dog.

Jack sensed she was down in the dumps and was still tired from the course and suggested they have a takeaway meal and open a bottle of wine. She was thinking good old Jack and said that would be lovely and felt a closeness between them, she then said she would go have a relaxing bath, wind down then come for their meal.

The evening went well; they watched a film, talked about old times and with their glasses of wine started to relax, it had been a long time since they had sat on the sofa together and felt that old closeness. Jack leaned over and kissed her gently on her lips; she could feel herself responding it felt good and she could feel those feelings coming back for Jack, he also felt his feelings rising towards her and pulled her into his arms and led her to the bedroom. That night, he was so gentle and caring, she was contented and enjoyed her night of gentle passion with her husband Jack.

Disappeared

Elisa had not seen or heard from her man-friend since the text he had sent her in London; she could not get hold of him by text or phone, she went daily with the dog to the park but he was not there in the usual place waiting for her.

She knew where his flat was but he had asked her not to come there as he did not want to raise rumours about them with the neighbours for them to think something was going on between them.

It was now over two weeks and she had heard nothing, so she decided to walk up past his flat with the dog; the flat looked empty no curtains at the windows; she thought maybe he was decorating, he did talk about painting the flat but he would have told me.

She decided to ring the doorbell there was no answer, as she was standing there, a lady came past and said, "No one lives there, the man moved out over a week ago."

Elisa said, "I don't suppose you have a forwarding address."

The lady said, "No, he was a quiet man and kept himself to himself, but I did hear someone say he was going to Canada as he had family there."

Elisa was in shock but thanked her for the information; she made her way back to the car stumbling, not able to see through her tears. "How could he do this to me, he was so sincere; he showed no signs of leaving when he was with me?" Even though he did feel guilty about Jack, he said he still wanted to be with me.

Elisa had to pull herself together before going home, when she got back, Jack could see she was visibly upset and went to her, holding her and asked what had happened. Of course, she could not tell him and just said she was upset about the dog walker friend; the news was she had died.

Jack seemed to accept her explanation and did his best to calm her down.

The weeks went by and she had not heard anything from her man-friend; he had just disappeared into thin air. She did not feel well worrying about what had happened; she lost interest in her beauty work; she no longer met up with the few friends she used to confide in, and she was now reluctant to even take the dog out to the park for its walks; she did not want to meet up with the other dog walkers; she did go a few times of hoping she might find him sitting there but it never happened. She was off her food and Jack noticed how much weight she was losing; she was having hot flushes and told Jack to stop worrying it was most probably menopause; she reassured him by saying she would go and see the doctor, but she knew being rejected this time had hit her hard.

Jack had been more supportive and caring since their night together and he had not thought about Sara so much. That weekend, Sara and their granddaughter called in to see them, still no sign of their son, but were given the excuse he had a lot of work on and taking the opportunity of the extra overtime.

Jack said, "Good for him, he needs to take it while he can get it because you never know what is ahead." He was thinking of his own position and his health did not think approaching retirement this would have happened.

Sara watched as he came over to Elisa and put his arms around her; she felt a sudden surge of jealousy and betrayal for what they had shared together. She looked at Elisa with hate in her eyes knowing what she did about her affairs, and yet Jack was still loving and caring towards her. She was thinking she could burst this happy balloon for her if only she knew, but she did not want to upset Jack. No, she would target Elisa and make her suffer as she felt she had more ammunition against her, but she had to bide her time when she was alone with her. Elisa just carried on day to day not knowing what was about to hit her.

Visit to the Doctor

Finally, Elisa was forced to go and see her doctor as she was rapidly losing weight, having flu-like symptoms, and hot flushes,; she thought the doctor would say it could be menopausal because of her age; she already had a hysterectomy in her twenties; she got over that quite well and over the years she and Jack had not had the worry of using contraception as they thought there was no need to take precautions and she applied that to the many affairs she had been involved in.

The doctor told her he would take various blood tests, and also arranged a breast scan and others to eliminate certain things; he told her the results may take a few weeks to complete but advised her to go on a special diet to help keep up her energy levels.

She ended up crying uncontrollably in front of the doctor and confided in him that she had been having an affair; she did this to unload as she could not tell anyone else, and how it had affected her when he had just disappeared.

The doctor also thought she was suffering from delayed anxiety because of Jack's brain tumour.

Weeks went by and then she had a phone call asking her to come to the surgery; she was also asked if there was anyone besides Jack who could come with her. Fear by now had set in but she did not want to worry Jack, she would tell him when she got back home, so she went on her own.

When she entered the doctor's room, he looked very concerned, so she tried to be chirpy and said, "It can't be that bad surely?"

The doctor then said, "Sit down, Elisa, I am sorry but it is not good news; you have got Aids." Elisa was in shock and at first, could get no words out and was thinking had she caught it from the man in Australia or was it from her latest man-friend who had just left her.

She heard her own voice as if through a fog saying, "I can't tell Jack." She heard the doctor say Jack must be told and he must also be tested to see if it had been passed on to him.

She was saying, "No, no, can't you just arrange some routine blood tests but don't tell him what it is for and if it comes back negative, he need not know?" By now Elisa was hysterical and the doctor was trying to calm her and said he would give her some medication to help her; he also said that Aids today could be treated; it was not always a death sentence and hopefully, she would respond to the treatment.

When she arrived home, Jack could see she had been crying and was waiting and wanting to know what she had been told; she knew she could not tell him the truth and told him it was a thyroid problem that hopefully they could treat with medication. Jack seemed to accept that and said we will get you through it and hopefully you will soon feel better.

But Elisa did not know that Jack had been having an affair with Sara, and he had managed to sleep with her again since the last time she had slept with Jack when she came back from her course in London.

Pressure from Sara

Jack had gone to the doctor, as he thought for routine blood tests and a general update on his condition. The doctor would have liked Jack to undergo more scans, to check what stage his brain tumour was at, but Jack said to the doctor he did not want to know because it would cause him more anxiety and he felt it was under control at the moment on the medication he was taking so it was left at that for the time being.

Sara had called in to see Elisa knowing Jack would not be there. She approached Elisa with a sharp hello and then said, "I have been wanting to talk to you. I have been hearing things about you with a man in London."

Elisa turned and laughed at her. "Yes, I was with many men in London on the course and later at the hotel when we all met up for drinks in the bar. So what are you implying?"

Sara was not going to be fobbed off and said, "You are up to your old games again seeing someone behind Jack's back and don't deny it, you were seen."

Elisa was trying to call her bluff and stay calm, but Sara was intent on goading her.

"A friend of mine saw you going to your room and saw you at the dining table with a man."

Elisa tried to think quickly and said it was a friend who was on the course and his partner was joining them later.

Sara was becoming quite brutal with her, calling her a liar and saying this friend had a photo of them together, and the man had been someone Sara had been having an affair with.

There was shock and disbelief on Elisa's face; Sara was just about to say she knew something was going on when in walked Jack; he was looking directly at Sara with a threatening look on his face as if to say keep your mouth shut.

Jack could feel the tension between the two women and thought it better not to interfere, he would hear Elisa's side later.

Sara was in a right tantrum now realising the man at the hotel was the one she had also been seeing; she had confided in him and told him things about Elisa and the suspicions she had when they were joking around and he turned to say to her, "She sounds very interesting. I would not mind giving her a go."

Sara had playfully slapped him and said, "Don't you get enough from me?" And the last time she saw him, she thought what a good time they both had together.

Sara had no idea that he had planned to bump into Elisa that day and knock her shopping over so he could get to chat with her, and Elisa had responded that she knew him from school and had fancied the pants off him then.

He certainly had been crafty the way he had played her, arranging meetings at the park to keep her interested all pre-planned by him and for her to arrange the weekend away.

But he also had to try to keep Sara sweet and give no hint as to what was really going on.

Sara had not finished with Elisa, and when she got a chance, she would tackle her and get her to admit she had been seeing her man.

It had been a few weeks since their confrontation when Jack had walked in on them and later had asked what it was, they were arguing about. Elisa innocently said she had been told that she had been seen with a man at the hotel when she was on the course in London and was trying to make a big thing out of it; she claimed a person she knew had seen me in the bar talking and laughing with this man.

She told her there had been many men on the course and the school had arranged an evening talk at the hotel and drinks later which we all attended. Jack seemed quite happy with her explanation and said he thought Sara had been very snappy lately and wondered if things were alright with her marriage to their son and how he avoided coming over to see us. Elisa told him things had not been good in their relationship as Sara had confided in her before she went to London, but she said not to tell Jack because she did not want to worry him.

But Jack was also thinking about how Sara had responded to him when Elisa was away.

Two days later, they received a phone call from their son to say Sara had collapsed and was in hospital and they were doing tests on her.

Elisa felt sudden panic and wondered if Sara had been having an affair with the same man that she had been seeing was he carrying the virus and if had he passed it on to her also. She could not say anything to Jack she would just have to wait till her son let them know the outcome of the results.

The Clock Is Ticking

It was like a time bomb waiting to go off. Sara was still in hospital, very ill and undergoing more tests. Jack was like a cat on a hot tin roof, very agitated and irritable not calm as he used to be when he knew Sara was going to visit.

Elisa still had not a clue about their affair and what had been worrying Jack was he had been told at one stage, Sara had been delirious and was calling his name and mumbling things unrecognisable to his son when he was at her bedside at the hospital; he was alarmed that she might say something about them sleeping together. He tried not to say too much about it so that his son did not question things.

Elisa was thinking again about the missing DNA papers and was sure it must have been Sara who had taken them and was biding her time to use them against her, but *where had she hidden them? Would her son come across them when he was sorting clothes to take to the hospital?* She knew she could not visit Sara at the moment because of how ill she was and because of the ill feeling between them on the last visit she made to see her and Jack.

A week later, their son arrived, as they were having their evening meal and as now had become accustomed to silence, they did not seem to have much to say to each other recently.

Their son stood there with a look of shock and anger on his face and said the results had come through on the tests on Sara, and then he just blurted out she has got Aids virus.

There was a sudden silence and the colour drained from Jack's face. Elisa was also shocked but inwardly thinking, I am not surprised especially as she had been having an affair with the same man she had been involved with, and was thinking it must have been him that passed the virus on to them both.

Their son was visibly angry and upset saying how could she do this to us. I know our marriage has not been good for a while and this was the reason she was having an affair.

Jack could say nothing as he was thinking about his own situation after sleeping with Sara, had he now got the virus; he would now have to go for tests and maybe will have to own up to Elisa he has been having an affair with Sara.

Their son suddenly spoke up saying, "In the hospital, she kept calling out dad's name and I just thought it was because she would come over to help to do things and look after him while you were away in Australia, I remember her saying at the park, a few times, so now I am thinking did she meet this person at a park somewhere."

Elisa suddenly jumped in and said she knew and Jack did that I go to the park a lot with the dog and meet up with other dog walkers, it could have been that was on her mind. Her son did not say much to her but seemed to accept that explanation. He then said, "I do not feel like visiting her anymore but if I don't, our daughter is going to wonder what is going on."

Jack then said, "You could just tell her the hospital has suggested no visitors for the time being as your mum is so ill."

Jack, the next day, arranged to see the doctor and told him what had happened and if could he undergo some tests to see if he had the virus, the doctor had thought Elisa had told him about her tests and was about to say something when Jack said you must not tell Elisa as I had an affair when she was in Australia.

The doctor then knew he could not tell Jack the results on Elisa which were unknown to Jack.

The doctor was thinking what a tangled web this all was, and he could not say anything, only to advise if he was to have sex with Elisa, he must now wear protection.

The Final Judgment

Sara after weeks in the hospital did not seem to be getting any better, so Elisa decided she would go on her own to the hospital; she did not tell Jack as he was feeling very low within himself and depressed since finding out the results of the tests and was unable to talk or tell anyone because they would then know about his affair; he became so withdrawn; he only spoke a few words to Elisa, but she put it down to his illness with the tumour.

She arrived at the hospital to find Sara had been moved to a room just out of the ward on her own; she spoke to the nurse in charge and explained she was family; the nurse said Sara was very poorly and not to stay too long. As she entered the room, shock went through her body at the sight of her daughter-in-law lying there. Sara was asleep so Elisa sat in the chair next to her bed for a while and was thinking *Why has it all come to this?* The time was going and Sara was still asleep so she decided it was time for her to go, as she made her way to the door, she turned and saw that Sara was staring at her, she whispered the words, *he has got the papers and said he will keep them safe*; she went over to her and said, "Who, Sara, who has got them?" But Sara had gone back off to sleep.

Elisa left the hospital with thoughts flowing through her mind. *I know it is not Jack, he would have said something and it's not our son he definitely would have created and would have told his brother. So it has got to be the man Sara and I were having the affair with.*

The next day, they had a phone call from their son to say Sara had suffered a stroke and things were not looking good.

Elisa thought the man at the park had left his home very quickly, and just maybe the papers could still be somewhere in the house; so the next day, she told Jack she was taking the dog to the park and might catch up with some of the others just in case she was out a bit longer.

When she arrived at her ex-man-friend's house and met the new residents, she explained to them she was a relative that had lost touch explained about some important paperwork she was trying to trace and asked if they had come across anything as he had not cleared the house just disappeared.

The elderly couple believed her and said they had found a box that contained utility bills and she could look through them and might find a clue to where he is. She found there were lots of old bills and some recent ones that he had not even paid. She was starting to feel despondent when she noticed a rumpled envelope underneath them and she recognised the writing as that of Sara.

She discreetly managed to tuck the envelope into her pocket, then thanked the couple for their help and said he must have taken the important paperwork with him.

When she got back to the car, she took out the envelope, the note was from Sara talking about their affair, but the bit that caught her eye said, 'I know you will look after those documents till we need them.' She had told him all about the things she had done even to the latest of what had happened in Australia.

This man now had control over her and when was he going to use it? Elisa was at her wit's end; she could get no more information from Sara. Jack was in a deep depression; she had no one to talk to; she could not talk to her son.

They had all been dealt with a no-end situation and a sentence on their lives.

And all because of the insatiable lust for sex.